MY NAME IS AMERICA

The Journal of Joshua Loper

A Black Cowboy

BY WALTER DEAN MYERS

Scholastic Inc. New York

Texas, 1871

April 30, 1871

When I got home from church Mama wasn't home and there wasn't anything to eat, which was strange because Mama always made something special on Sundays. The weeds in our little acre needed pulling, but I knew I didn't want to get out in the sun with no hoe. I had been laying low since Captain Hunter came to the ranch. Mr. Muhlen had hired the Captain to run things since Charlie Taggert, our boss, bought himself a place up in Montana. I guess the Captain was a good man if Mr. Muhlen hired him, but he didn't seem to have any use for Colored folks and he didn't mind letting us know. When he first saw me I was sawing down boards to fix the porch on Mr. Muhlen's house. He asked me who I was and how old I was. I told him I was Joshua Loper and I was sixteen. He didn't say nothing, he just turned on his heel and walked away without another word.

I was still running the Captain through my mind when Mama got home. She had been over to Mr. Muhlen's house. Mama had worked for him all her life. Before the war he had been her master, but 'cause he liked her he let my father, Nehemiah, buy her freedom and marry up with her.

"Mr. Muhlen wants you to go up north on the trail," Mama said. "Guess you better go see him."

I did not look too excited, because I could see Mama was not too keen on the idea of me going on the trail. I went over to see Mr. Muhlen and he said it was true what Mama had said. He was real short of hands and he had to get together a crew to make the drive to Abilene, Kansas.

"When we going?" I asked.

"Got to get the herd up by mid July," Mr. Muhlen said. "Sooner the Captain gets them going the better."

I said I would do my best. Ain't nobody who went up the trail was talked about like they was a boy. You went up the trail you were a man.

May 1

Mr. Muhlen had an argument with Captain today. Captain said he did not want to take three Coloreds on the drive. Mr. Muhlen said he didn't have time to find another cook so he had to take Isaiah and he might as well take Doom and me, too.

"Joshua is a good boy," I heard Mr. Muhlen say. "He's done some quail hunting for me and his mama is a good, religious woman."

Captain didn't say nothing to me, but Jake Custis told me later I was still going. I told Timmy O'Hara and he said that I had better practice my running because the girls in Abilene was so fast they would run circles around me.

Timmy was my best friend on the Slash M Ranch and I knew he would help me out on the drive. When he asked me if I was glad I was going, I said it was okay.

"If it's just okay," he said, "how come you grinning so much?"

Timmy was seventeen, a year older than me, and he had made his first trail drive at sixteen, the same age I was. He wasn't what you would call a good-looking fellow, but he had a look about him that made you think that any minute he was going to bust out into a smile. His eyes were kind of gray if you looked at them straight on and kind of green if you looked at them from the side. He said that was from his being Irish. There wasn't any question about him being one of the top hands even though he was young. He could get the job done and no matter what he had to chew on he never spit out a bad word about anybody. I didn't say anything to him about the Captain not wanting to take the Coloreds on the drive.

Mr. Muhlen called us all together in the afternoon. He said that it was important to him that the drive be successful.

"As you all know, Mrs. Muhlen is doing poorly so I must stay by her side. This is the first year I won't be leading the drive, but I have full confidence in the Captain to get things done right. If you boys get the herd to the railroad on time I'll give each man a ten-dollar bonus," he said.

I have never had ten dollars cash money in my whole life. Mostly we got either scrip money or just had what we was owed put down in the account book. When my father went up north looking for work he left us four dollars and that was the most me and Mama had at one time. Timmy had been on the trail last year and got paid seventy dollars cash money and said once he had a twenty-dollar gold piece. When I went to bed I dreamed I had a twenty-dollar gold piece and another one to give Mama.

May 2

The Captain had us branding today. He had me working like a three-legged dog at a rat hunt and was watching me with them dark rattlesnake eyes of his.

Isaiah was a big, broad man with a round face and the smallest ears that God ever put on a human being. He had been around and knew a lot about almost everything. He was born in slavery times and had worked for Mr. Muhlen before the war broke out. He stayed on the Slash

M, which was what the ranch was called, the whole time the war was going on. Isaiah had been a friend of my father's and when Daddy had to leave he told him he would not let me get into trouble.

I truly loved my daddy even though I didn't know a lot about him. He had been born free and worked for a Mexican before the War Between the States. Mama wasn't free, but when he asked Mr. Muhlen if he could marry her they made arrangements for him to buy her freedom. When the war broke out back in 1860 he left and went up north and joined the Union Army. He told Mama it was something he just had to do. I was only five at the time and didn't know much about what was going on.

After the war he came back, but none of the white folks near where we lived wanted him around 'cause he had fought with the Union Army. After a while, after he had been shot at by some Ku Kluxers, he decided to go up to Ohio, looking for work. He had a game leg from a wound he had got in Petersburg, Virginia, but Mama said he would be all right and when he found a steady job he would send for us. I knew he would, too.

Where Isaiah was big and kind of fat, Doom was on the skinny side and was all belch and bellow. My mama said you could give Doom a job eating raspberry pie and drinking store-bought coffee and he would find fault with it. He was twenty-one, and his skin was deep brown, about my color. His eyes was close set, which made him look a little shifty. I didn't know where he had come from, but he wasn't much in the saddle and didn't exactly cozy up to no work.

The cow hunt was already done. We had rounded up almost twelve hundred head and Mr. Muhlen had bought another thousand from some Mexicans. The Rio Grande was a little over a hundred miles south of us and it took them seven days to get them up to the range he was using. The Slash M range was about five miles wide with good grass and a stream that was truly sweet to drink from. The cow hunt ended two weeks ago and the regular crew has been getting them ready to go north ever since.

May 4

I am getting more and more excited and Mama is getting more and more down in the mouth about me going on the drive. Last year when I saw the guys leaving for Kansas I dreamed I was going with them, my hat pulled down low over my eyes and my wipe tied loose around my neck. Mama talked about farming and how good it was. I allowed how it was good, but what I dreamed about was being a cowboy.

8

Same day, evening

We spent all day cutting out animals that had not been branded, which was as hard a job as I have ever done in my life. We put the Slash M on their left hip and tagged their right ears with a square in the front. I was riding Pawnee, Mr. Muhlen's cutting horse. He told me to take Thunder, a dark red horse, and Slash, a real stout animal with a white blaze on his forehead, with me, too, so I had some good horses to ride on the trail.

I have had my own horse for a year. I was the one that caught him and broke him in and named him Pretty. Some of the old hands said he was too young to be a good cow pony, but he was all right with me. Mr. Muhlen had taught me how to hobble break a horse. Instead of trying to break his spirit, I treated him real gentle but firm until he understood that we were going to be working together. The hobbles let him know I could control him and he could not control me. He got used to them, so when I took them off he understood.

I did okay in the branding even though I fell off Pawnee one time. Pawnee knew more about cutting out than I did. One time I was trying to cut out a two-year-old longhorn and that animal was just determined to get back into the herd. Pawnee was cutting him and I saw the Captain watching me. That young bull moved back and forth and

Pawnee was moving with him. Then the bull made a real tricky move and Pawnee was just as tricky cutting him to a dead stop and I found myself sitting on a handful of air and grabbing for the horn. I bounced off the ground and got the wind knocked out of me and a sore backside.

Miguel came over and said that if I wanted to dig a ditch I would do better with a shovel instead of using the seat of my pants. I didn't appreciate that too much.

We finished the last few strays just before sunset and the Captain said we were going to start out on Monday morning soon as it made daylight.

Mama was a little upset as I thought she would be.

"Your daddy had to leave," she said. "You don't have to go if you don't want to."

I hated to see her sad, but being on the trail and being a regular hand was pulling on me something fierce. I knew I would do right by Mama and hoped she would be proud of the way I went on with myself.

On the Slash M Ranch there are only three regular houses. There's Mr. Muhlen's house, the bunkhouse for the crew, and our place in the back of Mr. Muhlen's house in what they used to call the Quarters. Mr. Muhlen came over to see me and told me he thought I would do just about all right on the trail.

"Your first trail is always a hard one, but you will come back a stronger man for it," he said.

Mama got me to praying with her and made me promise I would at least keep the Lord on my mind, which I said I would.

May 5

The Captain got the herd started at daybreak. I saddled Thunder, mostly because Mr. Muhlen and Mrs. Muhlen and Mama were there, and I wanted to look good. Thunder is big and I felt big sitting up on him, too.

"We're going to go with just two drags," the Captain said. "You boys slow us down and I'll drop you faster than you can spit."

Me and Doom were the drags, which meant we had to ride behind the herd. The Captain made it clear what we were supposed to do.

"Don't let them stop. Don't let them get out of line. And don't get them moving too fast."

The Captain was tall and so thin his body looked like a bow ready to shoot off an arrow in your direction. He was dark haired and his skin was tanned almost brown from being out in the sun so much. His eyes were a light blue and he had a way of fixing them on you that made you wish you could be someplace else.

In my mind I went over my gear. I had my rope, the Navy Colt which belonged to the ranch, a holster with cartridges, an extra pair of socks, an extra pair of drawers, a clean shirt, my slicker and tarp, a leather pouch that my daddy had given me, this notebook, and two pencils.

It was good seeing the herd moving out for the first time. As they started off, the riders moved closer to them and pushed them into a thin line, which made them naturally string out. When I saw Doom start I nudged Thunder with my knees. He didn't move.

"Don't go tearing him up with your spurs," Mr. Muhlen had said, "just let him learn you."

I touched Thunder with the spurs, just laid them against his flank. He turned back and looked at me like he was wondering why I had done that, and I had to smile. Then he started off on his own after the herd. I was going to have to come to an understanding with Thunder.

This is a list of everybody who is on the trail with us.

- ~ The Captain is the trail boss.
- ~ Isaiah is the cook.
- ~ Tim O'Hara and Little Jake are at the points. They lead the herd and make sure that everything up ahead is all right.
- ~ Miguel and Bert, the two Mexicans, are the swings. They ride back from the points and do a lot of the turning

and making sure that no strays wander into the herd and they back up the points.

~ Wade Mason and Bill Steele, who is just a little older than me, are the flanks. They watch the sides of the herd behind the swings.

~ Then me and Doom are the drags. Doom's twenty-one. His real name is Joe, and I don't know why everybody calls him Doom.

~ Chubb McLauren is the wrangler. He takes care of the horses. All in all there are forty-one horses in the remuda, which is what they call the horse herd.

I didn't want to turn to see if anybody was looking at me, but I couldn't help it and I saw Mama waving and it just kind of filled me up for a minute.

The back on my saddle was a little high and the whole thing was a little big for me, but I was comfortable as I settled into Thunder's rolling gait. As the sky lightened there were puffs of white fluffy clouds in the distance. The longhorns moved easily between the riders. The sounds of their hoofs drifted back to where I rode on the right side. We rode in pairs, one on either side of the herd. Doom was riding across from me.

By the time the sun had cleared the line of the earth, the dust from the herd had lifted. I saw Doom pull his neckerchief up over his nose and I did the same with my own wipe. We pushed the steers pretty good until the sun was high and I saw the chuck wagon go on up ahead, the mules pulling it swinging their heads from side to side.

We bunched the herd for their first break and watched them settle down peacefully. Isaiah made beef stew, which we had with rice and corn pone. It was delicious. I was tired and full of dust. Timmy came over and said all he could see of me in the morning was my hat sticking up on my head.

"By the time the sun got high I couldn't see where your hat stopped and your head begun."

I had been nervous in the morning, but when we got them on the trail again I was feeling okay. I left Thunder with the remuda and saddled Blade. Blade didn't like his cinch too tight, but I didn't want to fall off. I looked at Blade's back carefully before I saddled him and didn't see any sores.

We just about got going after the lunch break when some of the stragglers started drifting to the right. I went over and herded them back in line. But before I got the last one Blade bit at him. He went to the herd pretty quick then, but when I looked up I saw that the Captain was sitting by the side of the trail watching me. He didn't move, just sat tall in the saddle and waited for me to come to him. When I rode up on him he still didn't say nothing, just rode around the end of the herd and up the other side. I thought I could feel the way that man didn't like me.

The afternoon was pretty easy, but it was a long day. We rode from when the sun was high to when it was sitting just over the mountains on our left. I was tired and my back was aching and I was getting glad that the cantle, the back of my saddle, was high, because it was something to lean on.

We watered the herd and bedded them down for the night.

"Well, that's one day done," Jake said.

"The day ain't nothing," Miguel said. Miguel was Mexican but he didn't sound like one. "The first night out those beeves will spook if they hear a flea fart."

I didn't think they were going to be any trouble, because they looked really calm and peaceful.

For supper we had the rest of the stew, beans, and coffee and corn pone. It was delicious.

After dinner the Captain got us all together and made us sit in a circle to hear the rules we had to go by.

These are his rules:

Rule No. 1 ~ No drinking. Anybody caught drinking while with the herd will be fired. When you get to Abilene you can drink yourself silly.

Rule No. 2 ~ No gambling. Any cowboy caught gambling will get his time at once.

Rule No. 3 ~ No being stupid.

Rule No. 4 ~ No falling asleep on night watch.

"You better get all that down in your scribble book, boy." That's what he said to me.

I didn't drink and I didn't gamble, so I was not worried about none of that. I was going to try very hard not to be stupid or fall asleep on watch. The first night on the trail was the most miserable night of my whole life. There were four watches, starting at nine o'clock. The points had the first, until eleven. The swings had it until one, the flanks until three, and me and Doom until five in the morning. Then everybody had to get up.

It was a clear night with enough stars overhead to make you dizzy just looking at them. I was going to write in my journal but made the mistake of lying down to do it. I must have fallen asleep right away. When I felt somebody shaking me, I didn't know what was going on. "Get a move on! Let's go!"

For a minute I thought I had fallen asleep on watch, but then I heard the hoofbeats and I knew that something had spooked the herd and they were starting to stampede. Pretty was my night horse and I had tied him to a tree. I was on him quick and started toward the right side of the herd where I had seen a rider already up. I could see by the moonlight and I knew Pretty was surefooted, so I pushed him hard until I caught up with Timmy, who had reached the front of the herd. He was yelling and flapping his hat and I did the same behind him as we turned the herd left. They started turning and I let Timmy get a little bit ahead of me. We kept pushing them to the left. Behind me I heard somebody yipping. They went yip-yip-yip! at the cattle and I started doing the same. We pushed them left and then left again. When the cattle turned the second time they started to mill. I could see blue sparks from their horns hitting against each other. Then I saw that two more riders were up. I recognized the Captain coming toward me.

"Get away from the herd!" he shouted at me. "Back off!"

I pulled Pretty out and backed off the herd. I felt bad about the Captain yelling at me like that, until I saw that he was waving everybody back. The others were away from the herd, but they were still close enough to keep them turning into each other. I took Pretty a little closer. It took a full half hour of turning them into each other before the whole herd came to a stop. They were lowing and some broke once in a while but they didn't have no place to go because they were headed in different directions. The crew all spread out and just sat, nobody moving, while the beeves settled down.

It took a long time before they stopped moving around and even longer before they bedded down completely.

Wade came over and told me it was my turn to go on watch.

"You got five minutes," he said. "Maybe you ought to put your pants on."

In all the excitement I had got my boots on but not my pants.

Later, when Isaiah dished out the breakfast, he got on me about that. "Hey, Joshua, is it true you spooked the herd by running through them buck naked?" he asked.

Everybody laughed at that, but when we got back on the trail after breakfast I was feeling like a horse that had been run all night and put away wet.

May 7

The first two days were really hard. The Captain said he wanted to get the herd away from the range they were used to and accustomed to being on the trail. He didn't say anything about getting us used to the trail. If we have to push that hard every day — we must have walked them beeves thirty miles the first day and twenty-five the second — I think somebody will have to ride behind me and push me the way I push the drags.

At the end of the second day I was tired but kind of

happy I had done a whole day on the trail. By the time we bedded down about a mile south of the river, I was wondering how far it was back home. A long day like that in the saddle is no easy thing and then you have two hours guard every night. When I was on guard I sang, "O Mary, Don't You Weep," and I think the cattle liked it. The sound of somebody singing seems to settle them down, and most of the night you could hear somebody singing. Mostly, though, I was singing to me and Pretty. I wasn't used to riding in the dark and neither was Pretty, but me and him were friends, as much as a cowboy and a horse could be, maybe even more.

It was a year ago when I went with Mr. Muhlen down to Mexico looking for wild horses and he told me I could catch one for myself. I was pretty scared 'cause I had never tried to catch a horse before. We found a herd and Timmy and Jake helped me to rope the one I liked after we had run them into a little box canyon. He was snorting and darting back and forth and looking like he had a lot of life in him. We hobbled the horses we wanted to break and I kept a good eye on the one I had picked.

"They're only going to be half broke," Jake said. "You got to ride a horse every day for a while to get him really tamed down."

We got them back to the Slash M range and started breaking them. When it was my turn to break my horse my heart was beating so fast I thought I was going to fall out stone dead. Jake helped me to hobble him and I got a saddle on his back. But when I got up on him he threw me off before I even got close to settling in.

Mr. Muhlen put a man named Charley Pitts up on the horse and he rode him. He rode him again the next day and then the third day I rode him.

My horse was black and had a perky look to him, which is why I called him Pretty. Mr. Muhlen said he was too young for hard riding but might be a good cow horse one day.

"You treat him good and he will treat you good," Mr. Muhlen said.

Pretty is a horse you can talk to, too. I don't know how much he understands, but he sure acts as if he understands everything I say to him.

May 8

It was raining when we got up and the Captain wanted us to cross the river about two miles down from where we were. We got the horses moving and waded them over a stretch with a gravel bottom. Isaiah said when you crossed the Guadalupe River, which was the name of the river we waded through, you were officially on the trail. My butt was already sore from all the riding we did the first couple of days and I didn't need anybody telling me I was official. Isaiah made chicken, beans, and corn pone for lunch and it was very good.

Once we got across the river, we stretched them out and the Captain said he was aiming for us to make about twelve miles every day.

I was up on Thunder and he was a good horse, but he did not like me. I could tell the way he looked at me that he thought he was doing me a favor by letting me ride him.

May 9

It is a Tuesday and I have completely missed Sunday! I know Mama would be disappointed that I did not even take time out to say a prayer, but I will make it up. Today the light rain stopped and the dust from the herd came up strong. From where I was, riding in the back of the herd, I could see them stretched out for over a half mile. The dust lifted up like great brown clouds and drifted back toward where me and Doom were trying to keep the stragglers up with the herd. I kept my kerchief high, just under my eyes, but it didn't help much. I was breathing in more dust and dirt than I was stopping. I thought Doom was pushing too fast because he had some of the drags pushing into the herd. Billy Steele signaled us to lay back. The herd was stretched out and the cattle were walking along by twos or threes. I knew the Captain didn't want the drags going six or eight wide, which was what they were doing. But soon as you got some of the drags strung out they would slow down and then you had to push them again. Some of the drags were just weak and some were just plain not interested in being on the trail, which was why they was drags in the first place.

"What are you doing?" the Captain came and asked me and Doom when we had stopped for lunch. He asked us some other questions only he used some words that were not in the New or the Old Testament.

"What do you mean?" Doom asked the Captain. "We are doing the best we can."

"You run the drags up on the herd again and I will fire you on the spot," he said. "And maybe I'll shoot you to make it permanent."

Isaiah made stew and corn bread for lunch and it was good.

May 10

In the afternoon we kept the drags where they were supposed to be. It made me twice as tired worrying about what Doom was doing.

We went through some real pretty country, open mostly, with trees off to our left. The day ended earlier since we weren't pushing so hard, but the Captain didn't let us forget what had happened in the morning. He told me and Doom to get away from the fire because he couldn't stand the sight of us. Doom moved off by himself and I did the same. Timmy came and sat with me.

"I don't think the Captain will really fire you," he said.

"It wasn't me that was pushing the drags too hard," I said.

"All the same," Timmy said, "if he does fire you, can I have your leather pouch?"

"Before I give it to you I'll put it between two rocks and eat it myself," I said.

Timmy O'Hara was the grinningest man I ever knew and half the time he was grinning at me. I knew we were friends, but I did not like to talk about my being fired away from a job.

We bedded down on a high spot and it was grassy enough to please the cattle.

"I heard you singing last night and you can carry a tune pretty good," Chubb said. "Let's hear you sing something."

I had sung some in church and I liked to sing, but I was not no professional songbird. Chubb went after me again to sing and Timmy as well and so I said okay, and then I sang a song called "Just Before the Battle, Mother," which was a sad song but nice.

"You have got a sweet voice on you," Jake said. "If you weren't as ugly as a horny toad with false teeth I'd ask you for a dance."

May 11

I got on guard and I must have been half asleep when I got up because all of a sudden I found myself on Pretty and going along the edge of the herd. The night was clear and the sky was cram packed with stars. I didn't think another star would fit. I found the Big Dipper, saw where it was on the horizon, and tried to remember it so I would know when it was time to be relieved.

I hadn't had a real good sleep since I'd left home and when I did lay down and doze off the only thing I dreamed about were the drags, moping along any way they pleased just to devil me and Doom.

The way I had my horses lined up I would take turns riding Thunder, Pawnee, and Blade during the days and keep Pretty just for my night horse and sometimes ride him when I was feeling low. Four horses was enough to get us to Abilene if we took care of them and didn't ride them too hard.

May 12

I washed my shirt and laid it out on the chuck wagon so it would dry. We saw a small herd with four cowboys trailing them and Billy Steele thought they could be rustlers.

We got to a creek and we set down the herd, watering a few at a time. That was hard work because we had to get them to the creek, let them drink, and then get them away from the water so the next bunch could get to drink. The Captain wanted us to water the herd and then move across the creek before another herd came up on us. You could see the other herd's dust rising up about three miles behind us, which was too close for the Captain. Their trail boss had come up and the Captain told him to keep his cattle back until we were through and we'd clear out for him so the herds wouldn't mingle. That's what the trail boss does, look out for the herd and go ahead to find water and the best route.

It took us most of the afternoon to get the herd watered, which meant we had to trail the herd until just before nightfall.

The Captain had gone ahead and by the time we reached a small river the sun was just on the edge of the mountains in the distance. Jake, Billy, Bert, and Miguel checked the river and said that part of the creek must have passed over a devil's hole.

"A devil's hole can be a mile deep," Miguel said. "Can everybody here swim?"

Well, I am not a strong swimmer and I got to swallowing a little hard but I figured if everybody else was going to go across I was going to do it, too. Wade looked out over the water and said he could not swim at all.

"Don't worry," Jake said. "We will make you an Indian swing and you won't sink down into that devil's hole."

What they did was put a harness on a big steer and made two handholds behind it for Wade to hang on to.

"Hold on tight and you will be fine," Miguel said.

Wade took a hold and they gave the steer a whack and it took off across the creek with Wade dragging behind. When he got across, with everybody laughing at him, the rest of us waded across easy because the river wasn't any more than three feet at the deepest part.

On the other side, Jake asked Wade if he had went over the devil's hole and Wade said he was sure he had.

May 13

I know the Captain don't particularly like me and I don't make things any better. This afternoon a steer broke out of the line and started running toward a grassy hill to my side of the herd. Doom crossed over and pushed the line back so there wouldn't be a stampede with the other beeves following the runaway. I was up on Thunder and I went after the steer. It should have been easy, but then I remembered I hadn't done any roping from Thunder before.

The big horse covered the ground between us and the runaway real quick. I wasn't scared of his speed, but I was taken back a little. I got my rope and opened the loop and threw it as we came up behind him. Thunder didn't stop like a cutting horse would have and so I pulled up on the reins. The rope cleared the runaway's horns and I was wrapping it around the saddle horn when it went tight. Only thing was I got my thumb caught between the rope and the horn and I didn't know if I had that steer or it had me. I felt myself going over the side and I sure didn't want to be hanging by my thumb with Thunder pulling on one side and that steer on the other. The steer was jerked down and before I knew it, I was sitting on the ground next to Thunder trying to free myself. I looked up and saw the Captain sitting on his horse watching me like he always does when he's with the herd. I got my thumb out just as the steer stood up. I jumped back up on Thunder trying to ignore the way my thumb was throbbing with pain.

After I got my rope free from the steer, I herded him back to the trail line.

The Captain rode up next to me and didn't say nothing. He didn't have to. I pulled my hat down over my eyes and took my place on drag as the Captain rode away. I looked at my thumb and it was raw and the skin was scraped away. Timmy came over and asked me who had taught me how to use a rope and I told him I had watched a Mexican friend of mine, named Angel, roping around the Slash M.

"You got to tie your rope first like we do in Texas," he said. "You might want to practice doing that before you lose that thumb."

By lunchtime my thumb was swollen up bigger than two thumbs put together.

I was hungry and the beans, fatback, and coffee we had went down easy. I wondered what Mama would think about me sitting there and thinking them beans was so good. I'll read her everything I have written when I get home.

"What did you do during the war?" Jake asked Billy.

That was what they talked about a lot of the time, what they did during the war.

Most of the cowboys had been in the war fighting with the Rebels. Some of them still had their gray coats, which they wore during the fighting. The coats were old and pretty torn up — the war ended in 1865 — but they held on to them anyway.

"Not much," Billy said. "I was up in Tennessee, on Lookout Mountain. What we did there is to shoot at Yankees till we ran out of stuff to shoot. Boys was shooting scrap iron near the end."

Chubb, who ate more than any two men had ought to, was licking his plate like he was an animal. He asked Isaiah what he had been doing before the war.

"Worked for Mr. Muhlen for a spell, and before that I was busy working up in De Ridder, Louisiana. Worked lumber mostly." I knew Isaiah meant working as a slave, because he had told me before.

"Working lumber don't seem that bad," Chubb said. "I'd work lumber if they did it on horses."

"It wasn't so bad," Isaiah went on, "at least it wasn't so bad if the boss didn't have a bad day, or if he didn't lose at cards, or if he had plenty money jingling in his pockets."

"I worked for a man like that," Billy said. "If he had a good day he was all for shining his teeth at you and patting you on the back. If he had a bad day he had a way of talking through his teeth and was touchy as a rattlesnake sliding down a cactus plant."

"That right?" Isaiah asked. He started taking off his shirt. "How many times he take the whip to you?"

Isaiah turned his back and you could see the marks the whip had left. It made my stomach feel heavy and a cold feeling went all the way through me.

In a way it made me scared, too. Mama had told me stories about slavery, how people had been beat or tracked down by hounds when they tried to run off. It made me mad that people could do that just because you was black.

"Put your shirt back on." The Captain's voice was flat and dry. He looked hard at Isaiah and Isaiah looked hard back at him. Then he reached for his shirt and put it back on. When it was time to go back to work, I was glad.

May 14

I spent most of the morning thinking about Mama. When I left, she had told me to take care of myself.

"I'll keep your bed and stuff real nice," she said.

My bed was just some boards put together and some legs at either end to keep it off the floor. When I was younger, I wanted to sleep in the bunkhouse with the ranch hands, but when I got older, I was glad to have my own place with Mama. We had it fixed up pretty good with all the cracks stopped up so not many little critters could get in.

Sleeping outdoors on the trail was pretty good when it wasn't raining. Texas weather was good and warm. Jake, who was the boss when the Captain wasn't around, told us about a trail he had been on up in Wyoming.

"We got up near the Powder River and it was so cold the snakes all froze and folks was using them for walking sticks," he said. "The first night I was on guard it was snowing something fierce and I heard a howling sound and it sounded a little between an owl and a coyote. It was eerie and I kept my pistol in the holster, which I had hooked into my saddle so it would be right near my hands all the time.

"After a while I saw something coming toward me through the snow. At first I couldn't tell if it was a man or a horse. Then I saw it was somebody riding right at me. Well, that horse and that rider stopped dead still when I got near and I stopped dead still. We just sat there with me trying to make out who it was. I thought it could have been an Indian and I wasn't in the mood to have my hair parted from the underside.

"We sat there for a while with my heart pounding like all get out. Then the rider just disappeared. Poof! I looked around and didn't see him nowhere and I took my pistol out, ready for anything, but nothing happened. The next morning I told the boys what I had seen and they told me it must have been Little Tom.

"Little Tom was a Negro riding with the Goodnight Ranch. One cold night his buddy was sick, spitting up blood from consumption, and Little Tom decided not to wake him but to do two turns on guard. That night was the coldest night anybody had ever remembered.

"The next day they seen Little Tom sitting up on his horse, but when they went to talk to him, they seen he was dead, frozen in the saddle. When they went to tell his buddy, he was dead, too.

"They wrapped them both in ponchos, the white man and the Negro, and buried them soon as they found a place where the ground wasn't frozen too hard to dig in.

"But every once in a while up near the Powder River, you hear a sharp noise coming from around the camp — that's Tom's buddy. But if you see a figure in the saddle, you know that's Little Tom, still pulling guard duty on the other side."

I was glad that we were not going no farther north than Abilene, Kansas. I got to thinking about what it was like up north, being cold like that and everything. It must have been strange for the Yankees to come down to the South to fight in the war.

I remember Mr. Muhlen saying that the Yankees he met weren't much different from the Confederates except they all talked like they were afraid their teeth was fixing to break.

When I laid myself down to go to sleep, I thought about what Jake had said about Little Tom freezing to death in the saddle. It was kind of a scary story and it would have been just fine with me if he hadn't told it. I also thought about my father. I wondered if it was cold where he was.

May 15

It was Monday and I had let Sunday go by again without praying or even saying the Lord's Prayer, which I promised Mama I would say. I had been saving Pretty to ride at night or when we weren't trailing, but today I got up on him and I think he was glad. Nothing happened in the morning. Pretty had a little cough, which was probably from the dust which was as bad as it has been. It got up under my sleeves and itched something terrible.

One drag, which had a sore leg, kept stopping and Doom hit it with his rope. It got up and ran into the herd and I thought sure we were going to have a stampede, but the other steers just bumped and bellowed a little and things calmed down.

For lunch Isaiah made stew with carrots in it, which we had with grits and corn bread. That corn bread dipped in some hot lard drippings is about as good a taste as you can get.

"One time I took two thousand head all the way to England," Miguel said at lunch.

Miguel said he was 24, but he could have been 924 he had so many wrinkles.

"How you get them across the ocean?" the Captain asked.

"We didn't go that way," Miguel said, "we went by way of Indian Territory, then crossed them over the Ohio River."

The Captain smiled and I figured he must have had a better way of getting a herd to England.

May 16

We lost a whole day when the herd stampeded in the morning. They almost never get jumpy after a good night's rest, but they were ready to do something as soon as we tried to get them up.

"They look funny," Doom said.

They didn't look funny to me. I was saddling Blade and Doom was saddling this little red horse he liked when all of a sudden a bunch of birds took off from the bushes and the whole herd got to stampeding. Timmy and Miguel were up first and trying to turn them and me, Wade, and the others were up in a hot minute. We got the main bunch milling about two miles from the camp, but another bunch ran off and the Captain took Doom and Billy Steele to get them back. He told us to wait for him and by the time he got back, it was too late to make the distance he wanted, so he sat us all down for the day.

The thing was that the Captain was determined to make a fair distance every day. That way we would get to Abilene on time and it was slow enough so we wouldn't run all the muscle off the beeves and lose their weight. But that twelve or fifteen miles had to be spaced so they could get water when they needed it.

"A steer needs water more than it does food," Isaiah said. "So do people."

I didn't think I needed water more than I needed food and decided to go the whole day without taking a drink. I was doing just fine until the sun came up good. Then I took a drink before I realized I was even doing it.

Since we were sat down for the day, Jake had us getting wood for the wagon. Each of us went out and roped some wood and dragged it back to Isaiah. Doom also roped a pig. He said it was a wild pig, but the only thing wild about it was the owner, who came out and fired a shot in the air. Doom ran off with that pig squealing and bouncing along and the rest of us ducking for cover.

May 17

The Captain told Tim and Jake that he wanted to go twenty or twenty-two miles to make up for the time we lost yesterday. We got off to a good start. The weather was hot and by the time the herd was lined up and moving, you could tell it was going to be a hard day. The plan was to push until noon, without watering the herd, and to do fifteen miles. Then we were going to cut down the lunchtime and push for seven more miles before watering them and settling down.

"I once pushed a herd a hundred miles in one day," Billy Steele said.

"That's because you're a fool," the Captain said. That didn't set too well with Billy, but he bit his lip and kept his trap shut.

"You push a herd a hundred miles in a day, you got a stampede, not a trail drive," Timmy said. That sounded just about right to me and I was thinking that some of the cowboys on this drive were chewing more cud than they had. I guess if you didn't know a lot you had to make up stuff.

The beeves had worked themselves out where they all knew their places, or close to it. I was getting to where I knew which of the drags were going to give us trouble and I pushed them first so they knew they wouldn't be allowed to stay too far behind.

We had been out about an hour when we passed a cotton field. There was a group of Negroes in the field. They looked like a family, because there were children as well as grown-ups. There was one white man with them and he was sitting on a horse. It wasn't a working horse, just an old horse he used to sit up on while he watched the people pick cotton.

"I can't stand picking no cotton," Mama used to say. "God don't like evil and He don't like picking no cotton."

She had picked plenty of cotton in Mississippi. Even after Daddy bought her freedom, she stayed on with Mr. Muhlen and picked cotton and sometimes took care of the little children.

"When I seen Mr. Muhlen's daughter sitting on the porch reading from a book — just like she was grown — I was real proud of her. Ain't many peoples, even white, can read and write."

That was true. My daddy had taught himself to read and he'd taught me to read. Mr. Muhlen told me to go ahead and learn all I could, but don't be washing nobody's face in my learning because that is how people got themselves hurt. Isaiah said the same thing.

"A man who thinks he's too high and mighty is just looking for a hard fall."

I looked over at the Negroes picking cotton and figured

that they looked the same as slaves I had seen when me and Daddy and Mama were in Mississippi.

"You think they know they free?" I asked Isaiah when we got to stop.

"They ain't got no money and no land and no learning," Isaiah said. "What's free about that?"

I didn't know exactly what he meant by that, but he had a mean tone to his voice so I didn't talk on it no more.

Some folks got a way of letting you know they got a problem with you or what you're saying. Mr. Muhlen, when he gets mad, his lips don't move when he talks. Isaiah gets a deep, gravelly voice. The Captain always looks like he is fixing to kill something. He can look a hole right through you. Only thing I see is that he is moving the herd just like he is supposed to be doing.

When we got a little past the cotton fields, I turned back. The Negroes were still picking the cotton, only from a distance all you could see were their floppy hats moving through the fields. The white man on the horse had turned and was looking toward us. I wondered if he wished he could have been on the trail.

At lunchtime me and Tim and Miguel tried some left-handed roping, but none of us was any good at it. For lunch we had corn pone, rice, and strick-a-lean stew. It was delicious.

After lunch we had a hard time getting the herd up and on the trail because after going fifteen miles in the morning, they thought they were through for the day. In a way I knew how they felt 'cause the insides of my thighs was rough and sore enough for one day. I saw a wide-butted black steer push his rear end up and just leave it that way awhile before pushing his front legs up to a standing position. That was what I felt like doing. Since we usually only ride the horses a half day they were better off and ready to go.

Bert said he thought the Captain didn't know what he was doing, that he was going to wear us all out before we got out of Texas. 'Course he didn't say it where the Captain could hear it. We started out with me and Pawnee, who is a friendly little horse but skittish for no reason. What he wants to do is to work the herd. He don't want to just walk alongside of them, which is what we do most of the time.

We passed a stand of trees — birch, I think — and they made a pleasant sight. We also passed a family of five and they waved at us and we tipped our hats to them. They were poor white people and didn't look any better off than the Negroes. Before my daddy went up north he said that hard times was like the wind. It didn't mind who it blew on.

When we bedded down, the Captain came over and asked me if it was true that I was a good hunter.

"Passable," I said, not wanting to brag on myself too much.

"Then you go on over to where Chubb is sleeping with the horses," he said, "and get a rifle from the chuck wagon."

I got the rifle, a Sharps carbine, and went to where Chubb was putting up a rope corral for the horses and asked why I had to sleep with him instead of around the chuck like everybody else.

"'Cause Cap heard there was some people around stealing horses," Chubb said. "He heard that from some boys riding west of here."

"There's plenty of horses in Mexico," I said. "They should go down there and get some."

"Taking stuff you need is part of life these days," Chubb said. "Most of the land around here belonged to the Indians 'fore we took it. And most of the cattle and all the horses we're pushing know how to speak Spanish, so you figure it out."

"You think the Captain's okay?" I asked Chubb.

"Yeah, he gets the job done," Chubb said. "Since he lost his brother I guess the trail is all he got left."

"How'd he lose his brother?" I asked.

"Let me ask you something." Chubb got up on one elbow. "Did the Captain tell you to come over here and look out for horse thieves or come chew my ear off?"

I unloaded and reloaded the colt, then I checked my rifle. I didn't expect to get much sleep.

May 18

Too tired to write much. Chubb asked me if I was as good with a gun as the Captain says. If he thinks I'm good with a gun it's probably because Mr. Muhlen told him that so's he wouldn't mind taking me along on the drive.

A preacher on a buckboard met us on the trail and invited us to a church in Belton. He said it wasn't no distance past the Lampasas River.

May 21

I have never thought of shooting a man down in cold blood, but if I do shoot a man, it will surely be Isaiah Fatbelly Cotton. Either that or I would like to hit him across the head with a running iron and leave my mark on him. After two hard days of backbreaking work trying to talk sense to a bunch of sore-legged scrub steers and sucking half the dust in Texas into my chest, I got a problem with Thunder. When Chubb roped him for me in the morning, he was acting up and I had to hobble him to get a saddle on. The reason I wanted Thunder was he was a smooth-riding animal and wasn't as skittish as Pawnee or Blade. Pretty was smooth riding, too, but like I said, I felt better riding Pretty at night.

So I got up on Thunder and he acted like he had never been rode before and almost threw me off. If I hadn't grabbed the horn, I would have been throwed for sure.

"Get him, Josh," Timmy called out.

I held on as Thunder arched and twisted to get me off. He even reached around and tried to bite me. I'm real careful looking at the cinch so I didn't think I had fastened it too loose or gotten it twisted around to hurt him. Anyway, he bounced me around good for a while before settling down. I think he's just an ornery horse and gets a bit touchy if you get too comfortable riding him.

The reason I wanted a smooth-riding horse was because my butt was as sore as it could be. To make twelve miles north we were going every which way, maybe twenty miles of twisting and turning, to make sure we had plenty of grazing for the steers and drinking water. When we crossed the Brazos, which was muddy and dangerous looking, we had to ride up and down for an hour looking for a likely place to cross and just about had to give each of the drags their own personal invite to get them into the water.

With Thunder bouncing me around like that and all

the drags acting like they had their own timetables to keep, my rear end felt like I had spent six months trying to hatch a porcupine. When I unsaddled Thunder and did not see any sores on his back or any reason he should have acted the way he did, I told him he was a fool horse and should have been born a mule.

"You look like you got tailbone shock," Isaiah said when I got to the chuck. "That what you got?"

"I'm sore from sitting," I said.

"Naw, you got tailbone shock." he said. "Don't you think so, Billy?"

"You hurting on the sides of your legs like it's burning?" Billy asked me.

I told him yes and he said that it sounded just like tailbone shock to him.

"It ain't bad if you don't let it spread," Isaiah said. "You let it spread and all the nerves from your tailbone down to the back of your heels are going to hurt worse than a toothache."

"How you stop it from spreading?" I asked.

"Suet drippings," Isaiah said. "Hot as you can stand it."

He put some suet in a pan and heated it up and then told me to drop my pants.

"You don't want that to spread," Miguel said, looking real serious.

There's lots of things I don't know about and tailbone shock is one of them. I knew I didn't want it to spread, which was why I let Isaiah put the suet on me as I bent over the tongue of the chuck. It was an ordeal and I thought I knew what it was like to be branded.

"Now cover yourself real quick," Isaiah said.

I didn't have a problem with that because the position I was in was embarrassing.

"We got to tell the Captain we're going to be here a while," Chubb said. "While Josh gets the rest of the cure for tailbone shock."

"What's that?" I asked.

"You got to go and find you a black bear and have him lick the hot suet off," Isaiah said.

And with him saying that, they all commenced to laughing and rolling around on the ground like they had just heard the funniest thing in the world.

That afternoon, I was riding with a sore butt that was greasy and all the crew looking back at me and laughing.

During the night I told Pretty what had happened and I think he understood how low I felt.

Later I stretched out and I was beat down, disgusted, and sorely hurting and I didn't think that being a cowboy was the thing for me after all.

May 22

Doom asked me to read what I had written down in this book. I read him a page or two and he told me that I had only written down what had happened, like I did not know that to be true. Then he said I was a fool, because all he had to do was to remember what happened. He did not have to write it down. Daddy was right. Some people don't like you writing and reading.

May 25

I sat down to write two days in a row and just fell asleep.

May 27

It is raining something awful. I heard Jake say that we're moving toward Fort Worth and would get supplies. I would like to put my two cents in for a dry skin.

May 29

Delayed because of how high the river is. We got some supplies from Fort Worth and Isaiah made what he calls Son-of-a-Gun stew, which looks like it has a little bit of everything in it. The Captain went on ahead and we are to cross the herd as soon as the river goes down a little. The river is the West Fork of the Trinity.

A cow and a calf got into our herd and me and Timmy cut them out. All we had to do was to rope the calf and the cow came out after it. We tried to chase it away, but it didn't want to go. We were just about to shoot them when the owner, a farmer, came up and started flapping his jaws about us trying to steal his cow. Miguel roped him and threatened to make him a gelding and he was pretty glad to get away with his cow.

The rain got clear through my skin and soaked into my bones and I couldn't get warm for two days. When the rain finally stopped and the sky lightened up, it was the prettiest blue you would ever want to see and when the sun came out it lifted all our spirits. I was just glad to get out of my slicker, which weighed as much as I did.

Son-of-a-Gun Stew

2 pounds lean beef	1 set brains
Half a calf heart	Marrow gut
1½ pounds calf liver	Salt, pepper
1 set sweetbreads	

Cut up all meat and marrow. Simmer beef, liver, heart, and marrow in water for two hours. Then add sweetbreads and brains and simmer gently for another hour. Add salt and pepper to taste.

June 4

Sunday! I finally did not miss a Sunday and I said the Lord's Prayer. I wondered if Mama was thinking about me and wondering if I was saying my prayers. I felt good that I was.

Isaiah had some cherries he got in Fort Worth and I watched him make a special dish. First he took a good-sized tin of flour and mixed it with a handful of clear grease drippings. Then he took the pits out of the cherries and chopped them all up and mixed the cherries with some more flour until he had a roll of pink dough. Then he wrapped the roll in some muslin and boiled it. It was delicious and I am no longer the least bit mad at Isaiah. After dinner we sat around the campfire and had a good talk. Jake asked me to sing "Just Before the Battle, Mother" again. Since I was not in such a bad mood as I had been before, I did.

June 5

Yesterday we finally got the herd across the river. It was terrible. Jake, who is the boss when the Captain is not around, paid a man with a raft to take the chuck across. The rest of us had to swim for it. Jake had two steers who could swim good and he had them going strong, but then some logs came down the river and the lead steers stopped. Me and Miguel, who swims like he has some fish in his blood, were out in the water trying to pull that lead steer across. The herd started milling in the middle of the water and with me not strong enough to turn them in the water and too close to them to get out of the way, I was scared to death. I thought for sure we were going to lose the whole herd because the back end was still going into the river and the leads were not moving across.

Then Chubb brought the horses across a little upriver and the beeves started following them, which straightened them out. When I finally got across, I was wet from top to bottom and cold and suffering and tired out but I still had to help get the rest of the herd across, which took half the afternoon. All the time we were getting them steers across the river, the sky was getting dark and some big, dark, mad-looking clouds were drifting our way. I made up my mind that if there was a storm with the herd in the river, I would just cut out Pretty and head back home.

"What were you doing?" The Captain had gone ahead and found a place for the herd to go graze and we hadn't reached it. He was yelling at everybody and we were laying low. Jake told him we couldn't get the herd across the river. "We didn't lose none," he said.

That wasn't the truth, because when we took the

count, there were twenty-one missing and Billy and Doom had gone downstream looking for them.

"You are the sorriest bunch of sheep herders I have ever laid eyes on," the Captain said. He was looking right at me and I tried not even to think about nothing to say that would get him madder.

We bedded down the herd about four miles past the river and the Captain rode around them once and eye-balled them good. Then he told Jake he was going ahead to find a new place and we had better be ready to move out early.

No sooner was the Captain gone when Doom and Billy came back with twenty of the missing beeves. All told we only lost one, which wasn't so bad. Billy said he was hungry and went looking for Isaiah. Doom went around telling everybody what a good roper he was, like he caught the twenty beeves all by himself.

I was up on Thunder on guard 'cause Pretty was coughing again and sweating heavy from the flanks. It was hard to stay awake and I thought of the story that Jake told about the Negro who froze up at the Powder River. I sang myself a song. It started off being "Jeanie with the Light Brown Hair" but ended up being a song I was making up because I didn't know all the words.

When Jake got us up it was still dark and I didn't rightly know if I had any sleep or not.

By the time we could see daybreak over the hills we had the herd moving. Jake and Timmy started another count, but lost it halfway through when some of the beeves stampeded off to the left away from a jackrabbit.

We split the herd and milled the second bunch while Bert and Miguel kept on with the leaders. We got the stampede stopped but lost two hours while we settled them down. Then we pushed them up till we caught the leaders. By mid-morning I felt like I had done enough for the whole day.

We reached the spot the Captain picked out for us to noon the cattle, only it was two hours past when we should have been there. I didn't see anybody showing their teeth to the Captain.

Isaiah didn't have nothing to eat for us except beans and corn pone because the chuck had got soaked pretty good at the river. He wanted to ride over to a place he knew about near Denton to get some more grub and the Captain said okay and told him where to meet us.

When we bedded down, I felt sick. I cleaned the Colt and then begged some grease from Chubb to put on my boots to keep them soft. Then I fell asleep.

When it was my turn on watch there was a light rain and it was cold as it could be. Doom had showed me a picture he carried of the girl he wanted to marry and I sure wished I had a picture of Mama to take with me and I wished she had one of me, too.

When we got up in the morning, Jake was all nervous and I wondered what had happened. Isaiah was back and he made coffee and while we were drinking that we found out that the Captain found Bert sleeping on guard duty.

We held the horses while Chubb roped our mounts. That's when Jake told me that the Captain was putting me up on swing and putting Bert back on drag with Doom.

"You just watch Miguel and do what he does," Jake said.

I pulled my hat down over my eyes and hoped nobody would see me smiling as I rode toward the front of the herd.

June 6

"You ever ride swing before?" Timmy asked, forgetting this was my first time on the trail.

I told him no.

"The points got to stay in front and control how fast we're moving and look out for trouble and the best way to go," Timmy said. "The swings do a lot of the turning.

The lead cattle will usually go with the points, but some of the others won't turn if you don't make them. You got to make sure they don't split off."

Riding drag is bad because you got to eat the dust from the whole herd, but it's not that hard to do. Riding swing you had to move the herd, like Timmy said. Mostly what it meant was that you had to cut the herd, crossing to get their attention and then pushing them in the direction you wanted them heading to.

Bert was mad, but he was acting like he was mad at me instead of the Captain. He said something in Spanish just before we started moving.

June 7

Happy birthday to me! My last birthday Mama gave me a Bible that had been passed down from her grandmother and had a dried flower in it. I kept the flower in a chest for a while but then I lost it. Mama don't know that.

We got to a small creek and the water was terrible.

We had watered the herd earlier and it was just Isaiah that needed water for cooking. It looked clean, but I drank some, drinking it down without thinking, and then I threw it right back up.

We are pushing along good, but a lot of the funning we

were doing before has stopped. We got to a running pond and a farmer there said it was going to cost us a dollar a head to let our cattle drink from his pond.

"That's what he starts with," Timmy said. "He knows the boss won't pay that much."

The Captain came up to see what the matter was and Timmy told him.

"Or you can go on up about eighteen miles or so to the next creek," the farmer said.

He had two men with him. Both of them had rifles.

"I will make you a better offer than that," the Captain said.

"What would that be?" The farmer had his thumbs in his overalls.

"You let us water our herd here and I will tell my men not to kill you and your two friends," the Captain said.

"You can't just take a man's possessions," the farmer said, looking around at us. "And this water is my possession."

"Shoot the skinny one first," the Captain said. He pointed toward one of the men standing with the farmer.

The man did not want to have gunplay with us and threw down his rifle. "It ain't my water," he said.

We watered the herd with Timmy and Jake close enough to the farmer to keep him in check. When we left, we gave the farmer one of the drags.

"Do you think the Captain would have shot that farmer?" I asked Timmy.

"I would have," Timmy said. "You can't drive a herd without water."

Indian Territory

June 9

We waded across the Red River, but a big steer got bogged down and we had to rope him and try to get him out. We pulled and pulled but he didn't budge. Then we unhooked the oxen and tied him up to them and they pulled and we pulled and finally got him out. Then he stopped a few feet away like he was going to just sit down and be stubborn and it was all that we could do to get Billy not to shoot him. To tell the truth it was funny to see Billy get real mad, because he had a high voice and he kept yelling at the steer until he got hoarse.

We bedded down on some rolling grass fields and Jake said we was in Indian Territory. On the edge of the grass was some corn plantings and we kept the herd off of them, but Isaiah took some corn.

Off to the right we saw a church and there was a light in it. Wade, who was a churchgoing man, asked the Captain if he could go and see if they were having a prayer meeting. The Captain looked up at the sky and could see it was clear. He said all those who wanted to go to the church could go. Billy, Jake, Doom, Timmy, me, and Wade said we would go. The Captain said he would go, too.

"The Negroes are going to have to sit outside the church if that's what they want," the Captain said.

I did not like that and neither did Doom. Doom said if

he could not go in, he would not go to the church. I decided to go anyway because I knew Mama would have wanted me to.

We saddled up our night horses and went over to the church. It was painted white and the light glowing from it there on the hill made it look warm and inviting. When we got there, we found it was a Negro church.

"Come on in, children." The woman standing in front of the door opened her arms to us.

We all went in and found nine Negroes sitting inside and they were having a prayer meeting, and one old man held his Bible up and made a quote.

"And for thy cattle, and for the beasts that are in thy land, shall all the increase thereof be food," he said.

They prayed for our salvation and that we would be kept from all harm and we did the same for them. The white guys that came with us, including the Captain, showed a lot of respect for that little church. I think we all felt good when we left. Especially me.

June 11

Getting deeper into Indian Territory. The water is good here and so is the grass. Billy Steele sprained his ankle and Isaiah wrapped it with brown paper soaked in vinegar, which should get the soreness out. Wade had a birthday and now he is eighteen. He also got cramped up and had to take a dose of calomel. But that was not the big thing that happened. Last night I was drifting off to sleep when I found myself jumping up to stop a stampede. I don't have to know about a stampede for certain anymore. When I hear the hoofs going, even in my sleep, I just naturally get up and look for my horse.

When I was mounted I saw some other riders up and I thought it was our guys working the herd. Then I heard Chubb yelling, "Get your guns!" It was rustlers.

We went out pretty hard and I didn't know what to do. I heard the shooting and all and I did not know if I should try to mill the herd or to shoot at the rustlers. I could see some of them because the moon was as high and as bright as you ever want to see it. I figured the herd came first and I was riding as hard as I could, pushing Pretty to get near the front. For a while I was riding no more than a few yards behind one of the rustlers. I started yelling and bringing Pretty over close to the leaders. I didn't want to get in the middle of the herd but I wanted to cut near enough to turn the herd.

I got a few steers turning and they were piling into the ones on their left. My heart was pounding right along with the hoofbeats and I was pretty scared. Somebody came up on my right and I drew out the Colt and turned and saw it was Billy. Then I went back to pushing the beeves to the left. Billy stayed right with me and he was yipping and yelling right along. Up ahead I saw that part of the herd, maybe forty or fifty, had broken off. The riders going with them had more horse than we did and they were flying. I heard a bullet go whining over my head and I put my head down on Pretty's neck, which was covered with sweat. Then we heard Jake yelling, "I'm down! I'm down!"

Jake's horse had gone down and he was on the ground in the middle of the stampede. I knew that those steers could trample him and tear him to bits. Then I saw Timmy ride in, lean over, and grab Jake by the arm. Jake got up on Timmy's horse and the two of them were riding right in the middle of the herd with Timmy veering left the same as the cattle and looking for a way to get clear. His horse got bumped good and almost went down. It skidded around and came out of the herd hind parts first.

It took us another two hours to get the herd settled down good because they were really spooked and everything made them jumpy. When they were finally quiet it took me another two hours to calm down because I was more spooked than the cattle.

Wade and Billy had been on guard and it was Billy, with his high little voice, that told the story.

"I was just moseying along when I heard some hoofs from the right and I thought it was some of the cattle but then I heard the gunshots and I knew it was trouble," he said. "There were four of them and they came right at me shooting and hollering. I was going for my gun when they went past me and started stampeding the herd."

"You get off any shots?" Isaiah asked. He had made coffee and we were sitting around the chuck with a low fire.

"No," Billy said. "I was too busy getting out of the way."

"I heard a shot go past my head," I said.

"You got to have nerve if you are going to be a *bakaro*," Bert said, or something like that. "If rustlers come after your herd then you have to shoot them like you are a man."

I didn't know how many trails Billy had been on or how many rustlers he had seen but I did not blame him for not getting a shot off. I knew Bert was still mad because he was back on drag and I was up on swing, but I hadn't put him there. If the rustlers had come when he had been asleep on guard we might have lost the whole herd.

Nobody could sleep anymore that night and we did not try to. I thought a lot about how Timmy had rode through and saved Jake. He wasn't a point for nothing. Later Bert came over and asked me if I was sure that I had heard a bullet go past me and I said yes.

"You don't have to worry," he said. "They don't shoot slaves."

That got my jaw real tight. As far as I was thinking Bert wasn't worth the salt in his neckerchief. Later I told Pretty what he had said and how I was worried that we might have to get into it in a serious way.

When the Captain got back to the herd and found out about the rustlers he was madder than a three-horned bull with a toothache. He told Chubb to mount up and get his guns ready. "We're going to get our steers back," he said.

"Just us two?" Chubb asked.

"No, get the black kid," he said. "He can shoot."

Chubb asked me which horse I wanted. Pretty wasn't as fast as Thunder and he had been acting poorly. My throat was so dry I could hardly get out, "Thunder."

"Take this with you," Timmy said. He had got his rifle

and the rifle scabbard out of the chuck and I tied it to Thunder's rigging.

I wanted to tell the Captain I had never shot a man before but I did not think it would matter to him at all. I finished saddling up Thunder, cinching him tight to let him know this was not going to be no pleasure trip. He snorted and reared a little, but I jerked on his bridle and brought his head down. He reared up once when I was up on him, but I could not take any more time in dealing with his needs when the Captain and Chubb were already on the way.

We rode for an hour before we saw anybody. The guy we saw was an old man with bowlegs like a cowboy and dark squinty eyes.

The Captain asked if he had seen any riders headed that way in the last few hours.

"They're rustlers," the Captain said.

The old man looked us over and then pointed east.

The Captain tipped his hat and rode toward where the sun was still rising. We rode for hours with nobody saying anything. Once in a while Chubb pointed to the ground and I think he had picked up their trail. I looked on the ground and I saw some hoofprints, but I could not tell if they were our cows' or not. All I could think of was the look on the Captain's face and him saying I could shoot.

A little past noon the Captain stopped us. I was dog tired and the horses were beat.

"They got to be over that ridge," the Captain said.

The ridge was dark against the sky, about a quarter mile off from where we were. The Captain took his rifle from its scabbard and I did the same. We tied the horses just a few yards from the top of the ridge to a piece of stump. Chubb stayed with them for a while, calming them down like he always did, and me and the Captain crept toward the ridge.

On top he took off his hat and looked over. I did the same. There was a small creek, and it looked real muddy and shallow enough to make the rocks shine in the sunlight like silver dollars. There were cattle there, about forty head. There were also four men, one of them black, sitting on their haunches.

"Shoot the one with the leather chaps," the Captain said.

"Kill him?" I asked. The Captain did not say nothing, just looked at me with a look hard enough to light a match on. I checked the rifle and lifted it up. They were not looking our way, just sitting under a tree. The fellow with the leather chaps — they were slick and shiny — was nearest the tree. They were heating up some grub over a low fire, which they had shielded with a kind of tent so the smoke would not go straight up. I aimed real careful, first at his head and then for a little piece of the tree right in front of his head, close as I could without actually shooting him. Maybe, I thought, they would run off if they knew they were being shot at. I held my breath and pulled the trigger just as my daddy had taught me.

Soon as I got that shot off I saw the cowboy with the leather chaps fall straight back. He let out a howl like a hurt coyote and rolled over in the dirt. He was grabbing for his head and the others were grabbing for their guns. I fired off another shot, mostly because I was scared, and another one of them fell. The other two stood with their hands reaching as high as they could get them up. Chubb ran up and we went down to where they stood. The steers had started but they had been run too hard to stampede. They wanted to stay there with the water and that they did.

"Please do not kill us, boss," the black fellow said.

The Captain took their guns. Then he looked them over and said if either of them moved, to shoot the black one first.

I glanced down at the man I had shot and saw that he was still alive, much to my relief, and that I had only shot him in the nose, which was as big a nose as I have ever seen on something with only two legs.

The black fellow had just been nicked in the leg and looked all right. The Captain had Chubb take their saddles.

"Now you mangy dogs got one minute to get out of gun range," he said. "So you better run fast."

"I can't run," the black fellow said.

The Captain reached over and took off the guy's hat. "Shoot him in the head," the Captain said, "then he won't have to run."

They all started running, with the black guy limping and the other holding his nose. Then we mounted up and got the beeves and started back to camp.

By the time we got back to the herd, which was late afternoon, Chubb was telling the story like I had led the whole thing.

"He shot their big man through the nose, shot another one in the leg, and was fixing to lay the other two out right there by the creek when the Captain called him off."

Everybody was slapping me on the back and saying they knew I was a real man.

I got the runs real bad and when I was through with them I got up on my horse and thanked the good Lord that I had not killed nobody.

We moved the herd on with Timmy and Jake doing a count. Jake counts with his hat and Timmy counts with his head. They line up on either side of the herd passing through and when twenty cows pass through Jake drops a pebble into his hat. Then at the end he counts all his pebbles and the odd number at the end and that's how many beeves we have. After the count Timmy told me we had only lost five.

I was glad to see our brand on those steers because I wasn't sure if they were ours or not. When the Captain came up I asked him how he could see the brand from so far away as that ridge was.

"Tend to your business, cowboy." That is what he said and I did not ask any more questions. But later on I did ask Chubb when we were sitting around eating supper.

"Ain't nobody trailing no forty head," Chubb said. "And if you was, you would not need no four riders to do it."

I could see that the Captain still did not like me all that much, but when he needed somebody to do something he got me to do it.

June 12

Crossed Beaver Creek.

The Captain told us a story. This is the way it went. He started up the trail from Goliad in 1869 with two thousand head, all four years old or more and prime stock. He lost four hundred crossing the first river he came to because they stampeded off in two different directions, one

upstream and one downstream. He sent his men upstream because that was the bigger chunk of the herd.
They got them but when they went to look for the others
some Mexicans had drove them south and it was no use
chasing them. Then they lost fifty a day to stampedes
caused by thunderstorms.

"We lost two men, a pointer and a swing man," the
Captain said. "Then some rustlers stampeded the cattle
and when we went after the herd they got our horses.
Finally we crossed over into Indian Territory and the
Indians stampeded the herd. They killed old Bob Wilder,
one of the best riders you want to see. They took fifty
beeves and shot thirty dead. You couldn't shoot them
because they would ride hanging over the sides of their
horses and lying flat along the flanks and all the time
shooting arrows right through the beeves so they was
killing as many as they was taking.

"We lost some at the Arkansas River, some up in
Kansas, and I finally hit the railroad with three hundred
cows so run-down you couldn't a got a fifty-cent steak
dinner out of the whole herd. So I decided to winter it
out to fatten them up and every man that I had with me
quit except an Englishman named Jack Kelly and he was
not worth the droppings from a sick cow.

"Anyway the first snow came and every cow we had

died except one. I sold that one, gave the fifteen dollars I got for him to Jack, and went home."

"At least you had that one," Doom said, which, by the way the Captain pulled out his six-shooter and had to have his arm pulled down by Wade, was not the right thing to say.

June 15

I am so tired. There was a little blood coming from Pretty's left nostril. We're trailing along the Washita River, near Pauls Valley. I don't know how I'm going to tell Mama I have shot a man. Maybe I will not tell her.

June 16

Pushing on, but this trail keeps getting longer and longer and I do not get stronger as I go. Yesterday was hot enough to cook rawhide and I was hungry enough to eat it. Doom got a boil on his shoulder and was whining about it all day. Today I am getting soaked through and everything I have is wet and soggy. Isaiah is getting touchy and is serving up some bad food. We saw a herd of buffaloes today and there were two deer mixed in the herd. We also saw another herd of cattle. The Captain told us to look smart when some punchers from the other outfit came by. That made me feel good, him saying that. He had a kind of pride about us which made me feel good.

I spent a lot of time rubbing down Pretty, hoping to make him feel better, but I don't know if I am doing any good. I don't know if you should pray to God for horses. I prayed for Pretty.

June 17

The guys from the other herd came over and had dinner with us. They brought their cook, who was a Mexican and who laughed all the time he was with us. Isaiah did his best to outshine him.

The guys from the Circle N Ranch said that they came across four riders who had been ambushed by Indians just past the Red River.

"There was a black guy by the name of Ben Hodges who was the grandson of a Spanish something or the other, I think he said it was a grandee," the cowboy said. "He had two bags of gold dust with him. One of the other guys had been shot in the face, right through the nose."

June 18

Sunday. We woke up and Bert is gone. Jake said he collected his pay and went south. Isaiah said he was mad because he was on drag. Bert was a good rider and knew what he was doing around horses and around cattle. I felt bad because I thought the guys would think it was my fault.

"You don't leave a herd in the middle of a trail," Jake said. "That is something you just do not do."

We got the herd on its feet and I figured to fall back to drag because you need two guys back there. The Captain saw me letting the swing go by and he pointed up to where my place was and I moved up.

All the horses I was riding knew me now. Thunder still acted like he knew more than I do, but Blade and Pawnee were riding smooth as you would want. Pretty still didn't feel good and I told Chubb he was bleeding a little. Chubb said I had better watch him close.

The Captain fell back to drag and he started pushing the herd up faster than Doom and Bert had been. They had been more or less just making the drags stay up with the herd the way they was supposed to, but the Captain was pushing us all. We had to ride a little faster and a little better because he was back there. He could ride, too.

Sometimes I watched him and I never saw anybody ride without using his hands the way he did.

We got to the Canadian River at ten in the morning. Timmy and Jake cut out the good swimming steers and pushed them straight into the river. Me and Miguel went across with the first steers with Wade and Billy pushing right behind us. When I got across I rode up ahead a little and got on some high ground and looked back at the steers in the water. The sun on their horns was a wonderful-looking sight. Then I saw some of the cattle milling and got out of my daydream. I pushed hard down to where I could get them moving again before the Captain noticed.

I was thinking back about him telling me to shoot the rustler and wondered if he minded that I did not kill him or if he would have felt bad if I had killed the fellow. I truly do not believe it would have made a difference to that man.

We got the herd across the Canadian and moved them a few miles away from the river to let them graze. The count was good. We had not lost any during the crossing. Everything looked okay and the Captain had the points and Doom hold the herd while the rest of us went back to get the chuck wagon.

"How can you break a chuck when you were on the ferry?" Billy asked. That was true. The man who had the ferry had taken Wade, Isaiah, and the wagon across.

"We came up the hill over there," Isaiah said, pointing to a real little hill, "and the mules ran over a rock and just busted up the front of the wagon."

It was busted up bad. We looked around until we found a tree about the size of the wagon tongue and we pointed it out to Isaiah, who said we should get off our horses and help him cut it down. We did not. He got out his saw and started hacking and cussing. Isaiah said he was a religious man but he knew more cuss words than anybody I had ever heard before. I covered up Blade's ears because some of those cuss words mentioned horses. When Billy saw me do this he covered up his horse's ears and that made Isaiah even madder and then some of the curses got to talking about us.

When he finished cutting that tree down and trimming off the branches, we roped it and drug it back over to the chuck. Wade and Billy tied the trunk to the broken tongue and that was good enough until we got back to camp.

Isaiah made coffee and we caught a wild turkey but did not get to eat any of it then because the Captain wanted us to move on, which naturally we did. You do not say no to that man. In the afternoon he put me back on drag and he told me to keep my eyes open.

"I do not expect any Indian trouble," he said. "But if we get any you better be ready."

I knew two Indians. My cousin Belle had married an

Indian boy by the name of George Brown. His Indian name was something like Little Bird or Little Owl, something like that.

The other Indian I knew was named Two Hearts. I asked him what that meant and he said it meant it was his name. Then he asked me what Joshua meant. I told him it meant "brave warrior."

We found a puncher riding a little past the camp and he asked us if we needed a rider. He looked old, maybe thirty or even older — he had one of those droopy mustaches and was so skinny he'd have to stuff feathers in his shirt to cast a shadow. The Captain took him on and put him up on swing, which made my jaw tight because I thought he should have put him back on drag and let me handle swing.

June 20

I am tired right through to the bone. A lot of the stuff I had to think about when we first began I don't have to think about anymore, it just comes natural. When the herd starts getting out of line I don't think about what to do, my legs just move and my horse starts to push them back in line. Sometimes at night when I'm on guard it seems like I can feel things in the dark. I know what sounds are trouble and which are probably just a lonely coyote howling at the moon. A lot of things I would like to think about I can't bring my mind to. I was still mad about being put back on drag but I didn't want to say nothing because nobody likes somebody all the time complaining. When I was on guard I told Pretty about me being on drag again. I didn't make that big a thing over it because I knew he was still feeling poorly, too.

June 21

Spent some time with Timmy showing me how to tie down my rope in a hurry. He said if I lose my thumb by trying to rope like the Mexicans we could put it into some beans for flavoring. I told him if I had a spare minute or two I would see if I could muster up a chuckle from that.

Afternoon

This was our worst stampede yet. The Captain said we had to graze the animals forward and not let them drift back, because we were losing a mile at every grazing time. That meant you could not let the animals graze free but had to be up on your horse and pushing them a little even when they thought they had some time off. Maybe that was why they stampeded. Sometimes you cannot tell why they go, but they went.

They were moving fast, their hoofs drumming along the flat ground, and we went after them. I was up on Pawnee, who could run hard for a short distance, but he wasn't the horse for a long haul. Timmy was up on his best horse and he was trying to turn the leads and I saw he was having a hard time. Billy went by him and was riding next to a steer and kicking at it with his left leg. Least that is what he looked like he was doing. He got that steer turning and him and Timmy got them pointed west and Wade swung around them and started the first turn in. Me and Pawnee come around and between us all we had them pointed south, but the back steers had their mind set on going north. Timmy was swinging his horse back to cut off the beeves that were not turning and he and Miguel were waving their hats and shooting and doing everything they could to get that stampede stopped. Doom was turning them from the outside, but that got Timmy and Miguel cut off and Miguel's horse was spinning so, I thought he would go down.

You don't want no horse tangling with a steer's horns and I was moving Pawnee out of the way the best I could. The dust was coming up so fast I started choking and pulled my kerchief up over my nose with one hand while

I was guiding Pawnee with my knees. I came real close to falling off and I swear Pawnee caught me himself.

Jake and Wade and even Chubb was off on the right and I saw they was trying a wider mill. I got Pawnee out where I could join them and Miguel and Timmy did the same. Finally we got a wide, loose kind of milling, which is dangerous because they was so loose they could have stampeded again easy. But once we got them near to stopped we moved in on them and herded them together in a jumble until they had stopped good.

"Where's the new guy?" Doom asked.

I got a sick feeling in my stomach, but I did not say nothing. We moved away from the herd and watched it. We saw a little commotion on one side and some beeves moving away from a spot and bellowing. Wade went into the herd and it was him that found the new guy.

There was not much of him left. It was all white meat and bone and you could not even tell where his left arm had been. The only way you knew it was a cowpuncher was the boots. They were mashed good, but you could still see they were boots.

We got his slicker and gathered him up in it. The cattle had just stomped him to death and had ground all his insides into the ground. The horse he was riding was dead, too.

Chubb, me, and Isaiah dug a grave and we laid the

cowboy in it. I made a cross out of two branches tied together with some rawhide and put it at the head of the grave. We took our hats off and the Captain prayed over him and I thought he meant every bit of it. It made me think that maybe I did not know the Captain as much as I thought I did.

I had been mad at the guy because he was riding swing when I thought I should have been. Now I felt bad that he was dead. I was too ashamed to ask if anybody knew his name. I found out later from Jake that he had been called Liam, which was an Irish name. Then we got the herd strung out and moved on.

When we bedded down nobody talked about what had happened, but it was with everybody. Stampedes could happen any minute and you could lose your life as easy as the cowboy did that afternoon and we all knew that. We were all down in spirit and when Isaiah asked me to sing a song I didn't want to, but then Timmy asked me, too, and so I sang "Just Before the Battle, Mother" again. Chubb joined in and when we got to the part that goes "Do not forget me, Mother, if I'm numbered with the slain," it was almost too sad to bear.

June 22

I have finally figured out what this trailing is all about. It is about riding a horse slowly alongside these cattle for mile after mile and making sure they don't have to work too hard. Then it's about making sure they have enough grass to graze on even though you are too tired to scratch where you itch. It's about making sure the beeves don't get too thirsty even if all you have to drink is water so foul you got to strain it through the sweat of your neckerchief. It is about making sure their feet don't hurt them, or nothing gets their stomachs upset, or upsets whatever it is steers dream about. Last it's about calming them down every night and singing to them so they don't feel lonely, even though you have not seen the ones you love for weeks.

Tonight on guard I sang "Lorena" to them. It is the prettiest song I know and I think they liked it. Maybe tomorrow I will dance a waltz for the drags.

June 23

A band of soldiers come by. We all wanted to get a good look at them and when we did we saw they were all black with just a few whites. They were riding some fine-looking horses and they were some fine-looking fellows.

A white soldier came over to where we were camping. The Captain went into the chuck and when the soldiers came over they went up to Jake, who had stood up and was talking to him.

There was something about those black soldiers that was special. They carried themselves like they owned the world. I wondered if my daddy had looked like that, all clean and polished up with shiny boots and a clean uniform. They knew we were looking at them hard and they strutted. One got off his horse so slow he could have been a picture that was moving instead of a man. That horse never moved an inch.

Then the Captain came out of the chuck and I saw he had put on a jacket from a uniform, only it was gray. He pulled it down in front and it was a pretty good-looking uniform, too.

"Timmy, what's going on?" I asked.

"They're Buffalo Soldiers," Timmy said. "A lot of them fought in the war."

The Captain had on the jacket from his days in the war, too. The war was over, but they were still facing each other off. The feelings were still hard, even as it had been for my daddy.

One of the black soldiers came over and saluted the Captain, but the Captain just looked him down.

The white soldier — I figured he was in charge — said

something and in a flash all the blacks were back on their horses and moving out. The white soldier turned and saluted the Captain and the Captain gave him a salute back. As the soldiers went off I saw the Captain watching them. He didn't take off his uniform jacket until they were out of sight.

Pretty was bleeding from the nose again and Chubb said I had better take a good look at him. I went out to the remuda and roped Pretty. It was easy to rope him because he did not move. A little roan was pushing at him and I hit the roan across the face with my rope, which was the wrong thing to do. That roan was Miguel's horse and I know he would not have taken kindly to my hitting his horse. Pretty can't hold a bit and Chubb said he was slowing down the remuda. I thought he might need worming and begged some rough-cut tobacco from Isaiah and tried to get Pretty to take that, but he would not.

"How much will it cost to take him to a horse doctor when we reach Abilene?" I asked Chubb.

"Two dollars," Chubb said. "Maybe three dollars with the prices they charge in that town."

"Then I will take him to the best doctor in the town when I get there," I said.

"The Captain says he ain't pulling his weight," Chubb answered.

That was not true. Pretty was sick, but I knew he was a

good horse and the best friend I had next to my mother, Timmy, and maybe Isaiah. He was even a little bit before Isaiah.

When we bedded down and I went to the remuda, Chubb asked me if I wanted him to rope Pawnee for my night horse and I said no.

"Pretty will do," I said.

He sent me a hard look and I sent him one right back.

June 24

Last night the sky was full of stars. It looked like they were crowding each other, tumbling and sparkling in the night sky so far away and at the same time getting inside of you and filling you up with the feeling of bigness and how open it all was. I felt like I could open myself and get as big as the sky.

I told Pretty to look up and pulled his head so he could see all the stars twinkling so bright against the deep black sky. I knew horses could see lightning jagging across the skies, but I wondered if they ever just looked at how wonderful the stars looked at night. I hadn't tightened his headgear and Pretty had spit out the bit, which I knew he would. But I did not try to push it on him.

The way we guard the herd is that one rider goes

around one way and the other goes around the other way. Then we usually meet at the same place. But Pretty was barely dragging along and when I didn't meet up with Doom in the regular place he asked me what was wrong. I just told him he should tend to his business and I would tend to mine.

Miguel and Billy got into a shout out and they would have had a fight but they were both too tired and said they would settle it in Kansas. The Captain said if they got into another argument on his drive he would settle it by shooting the ugliest one.

Then we got into a funning thing about who was the ugliest, Miguel or Billy, and Timmy said it was a good thing they did not include Isaiah in the ugly contest because he was the winner by a head and a neck. That got Isaiah's jaws tight and I stayed out of it.

The night come and we had sour beans and gristle and dry pone, which was the worst meal we had ever had on the trail and maybe the worst meal I had ever had in my life. I asked for seconds and the seconds was as bad as the first.

June 25

Indians! Timmy held up his hand to stop the trail, only he held his hat up, too, and waved it, which meant that there was either trouble or riders ahead. What there was was Indians. They came over the ridge riding a bunch of small horses, some of them pintos. They rode bareback and rode good, like they knew what horses were all about.

Two rode up to Timmy and the others, about thirty of them, rode in between us. There were three between me and Miguel, three between him and Wade, three between him and Timmy, and the same thing on the other side. I got a funny feeling in my stomach and my mouth went dry.

I looked over to where the Captain was and he was sitting tall like nothing was going on. I pulled my hat down over my eyes and pulled my neckerchief up in case they stampeded the herd and I had to ride through the dust to get them back under control. The Indians who were talking to Timmy pointed at the herd and then made a circle over his head. I did not know what that meant.

Timmy wheeled his horse around and came back to where the Captain was. They talked a little and then the Captain turned and pointed to Wade, me, and Miguel. We went over to where him and Timmy was.

"Osage Indians," he said.

"They said they want fifty beeves to pass through their land," Timmy said. "They also said if we are better riders than they are we can go through for free."

"They're probably just hungry," the Captain said. "But we better be ready for a fight. Let's go talk to their leader."

Their leader was stoutly built with a round chest and a lean, hard face. He wore beads around his neck and a leather vest and leather pants. His horse did not have a saddle, just a blanket, and it did not look like that good a horse. He had two feathers on a band around his head and a rifle tied behind his back.

"You want to go to war with us?" he asked. His voice was calm, like he was asking for a cup of coffee or the time of day.

I looked at the Indian and he smiled. He moved his horse next to the Captain and looked into his eyes. There was no fear in the Indian's eyes and I did not see fear in the eyes of the Captain. Then the Indian moved his horse next to mine. He came as close to me as he could and leaned over and put his face real near mine. Then he looked at me and stared me right in the eyes and I did not know what to do. I lifted the Colt from the holster and he looked down at it. When he looked back into my face it was with cold eyes and a cold heart.

"Fifty cattle," he said.

"Two steers," the Captain said.

"I will come back with all my braves and kill all of your cattle," the Indian said.

"Have them bring shovels," the Captain said. "Those we don't feed to the cattle we can bury."

"Eight head," the leader said.

"Two," the Captain said. "No more."

The Indian turned his horse, called out something to his braves, and they cut out two steers — two fat ones — and drove them off.

"Stay alert," the Captain said.

He did not have to tell me that.

The leader came back and told the Captain we were near his village. "You can pass."

Then they left.

"He was lucky he settled for two," Chubb said when they had left.

"We were lucky they didn't decide to kill us and take them all," the Captain said.

June 26

Up on Pawnee. As we get farther north we see more herds. There must be at least two clouds of dust in plain sight every day. The land up here is different from Texas.

It looks like nobody has hardly been here. We don't see many people and no roads to speak about. Today I was almost too tired to write again, but then two things happened. The first was we saw a herd of about fifty antelopes. Seeing them made me feel real good.

The second thing that happened was in the evening. We had bedded down when two riders from the Diamond K Ranch came by.

"We heard you had a reading Negro over here," one of them said.

I don't know where they heard that I could read, but they brought a paper with them that had come all the way from California. It was called the *Marysville Daily Appeal*. Everyone sat around and I read aloud from the three stories they had marked off to see if I could read them. One was about the celebrated horse Richmond. I guessed Richmond was his name. He was a stud horse and they gave his height as seventeen hands and his weight at 1,405 pounds. That is some big horse! That meant his withers were exactly as high as me, which is five feet eight inches tall. I don't know what they were celebrating.

Then there was a story about somebody named Darwin, who had a theory that somebody had an ancestor who was part monkey. When I read the part that said the monkey would "sit in a chair, smoke his pipe, and drink rum like a man," Chubb said that he did not believe a word of it and wanted to see it for himself even though he could not read it.

The last story was about how they were going to bring fifty thousand Germans to Oregon. Wade did not think they could fit that many Germans into Oregon and even if they did he did not know why would they want to.

After I had finished reading the three stories the boys from the Diamond K said that it was sure true that I could read. Then they sat down and grubbed with us and everybody talked about those stories, especially about how big that horse was.

Later, when they had gone, Isaiah came over and said he was proud of me being able to read and though I didn't say nothing I felt the same way.

June 27

Isaiah asked me and Doom to gather up some cow chips for the fire and said he would give each of us some extra dessert if we did so. I said no because I was not hired to gather up cow chips. Doom, who would do anything for something extra to eat, said he would.

Working a trail was hard work. If the wind was at your back it was hard because you were up all day in the saddle with your hind parts burning and your back hurting and maybe other parts sore from being half crushed by a big, ugly steer or a burn from a rope sliding over your palm. But when the wind is blowing in your face and you are eating dust from sunup till sundown and your eyes are feeling gritty, it gets even worse. On top of all that Isaiah wanted us to get him some more cow chips.

We pushed real hard to get to a creek the Captain knew about near the Salt Fork of the Arkansas River. He did not want to cross the river with the cattle wanting to drink. When we stopped and the Captain had planned his next day's trailing he gave us the rest of the day off, which was almost two hours before we were supposed to bed down.

"Do you think Cap is going soft?" Timmy asked. "With two hours off we might get fat and lazy."

"If you had seen him with his brother you would think he had a kind heart and a big one, too," Chubb said.

I was fixing to ask him about the Captain's brother when the Captain came over and sat just away from the fire. Then Doom, who has the habit of being loose lipped, started talking about how we were being pushed too hard.

"Cowboys need rest," he said, looking around at all of us.

We found other places to rest our eyes because we did not think the Captain was going to be pleased with Doom's jawboning.

"You ain't a cowboy, you are just a boy," the Captain said, looking a hole through Doom. "And as softheaded as you are, somebody will probably shoot you and put you out of your misery and then you can have as long a rest as you want."

Then the Captain got up and walked away. Things got so quiet you could hear a cricket blink and though we were all tired there wasn't a man there who would not have rather drank possum pee than get the Captain mad.

Evening

After we ate, Isaiah took the chuck and said he was going to look for a Colored town he knew about. Timmy went with him. They wanted to buy flour and fresh eggs, which was all right with me. The Captain said that the rest of us should wash and clean ourselves up because the steers was complaining about the stink.

"And make sure you wash your socks," he said.

In truth, I was dirty. We got into a pond and washed down good and I even used a piece of Pears' Soap that smelled like it had been perfumed. I had the soap after

Wade and Billy, but Chubb said he did not want to use the soap because it smelled like something a woman would use.

Sometimes, on the range, you would have a steer that wanted to go his own way. He wouldn't want to stick with the herd. Chubb was a little like that. There were more things he was trying to stay away from than things he liked.

I decided to wash my clothes and my socks and I did that and laid them out on the ground under a tree and then Jake said that the cattle were drifting back so we had to put on the wet clothes and go push the cattle up. A herd could drift back two miles as they bedded down and that would just be two miles you had to make up the next day.

Doom told me he was ready to collect his money and go home, but he was afraid to ask the Captain.

When I finished my guard I barely had time to stretch out good and find a new place that hurt before Jake was getting us up. Timmy and Isaiah had not got back yet and all we had to eat for breakfast was whatever we had in our saddlebags, which in my case was just a string of beef jerky. I made some coffee with the leftover grounds from Billy's makings and it tasted like horse sweat and toe jam, but it was hot.

June 28

The Captain told me to lag behind and to let Doom push up the drags. I asked him why.

"In case there is an ambush from behind by Indians, they will kill you first and we will hear you screaming and save the cattle," he said.

He put me back there looking out for Indians. I now had a reputation as a shooter and a reader and I don't know which was worse.

"Sometimes you have to kill Indians," Billy said when we were nooning the beeves. "Indians ain't like white men."

"Indians are different," the Captain said. "If you ride on their range and shoot their buffalo they have a way of not liking it. Then soon as you shoot a few of them and then tell them that you are taking down their homes they get mad again. They're touchy that way."

"That is not fair," Jake said. "We should not shoot them for no reason."

"Lots of things ain't fair in this world," the Captain said. "When you want things to be fair you put on the saddle and let your horse ride you a while."

When the Captain said that, I thought about Pretty. What I thought was that I didn't know what a horse thought was fair. The thinking didn't last long because of how tired I was.

June 29

There was a small bunch of beeves on the right of the herd as we passed by a stand of cottonwoods and you could see them edging over to our trail. From where I was on drag I could see Billy trying to shoo them off, but they kept coming. The only thing to do when you get a few beeves like that is to let them come along and figure out who they belong to later. But Billy did not want them in the middle of our herd.

I went up and got them. There were nine altogether and by their ear markings I knew they did not belong to anybody I knew.

"They belong to Jenkins," Billy said.

Jenkins had a big herd of over two thousand animals up ahead of us and I pushed his nine beeves onto the end of our herd.

They were good-looking animals and weren't anybody's drags and they were soon finding better spots for themselves.

The thing was everybody was pushing their herds to get them up by July. It could take anywhere from two and a half to three and a half months to get a good-sized herd up the trail. If they got them up by July then they could go back and maybe get another herd up before the real bad weather hit.

June 30

Got leg cramps something awful. I let out the stirrup straps so I could stretch my legs and Timmy asked me if it really took a hundred miles of pain for me to figure that out, which I did not appreciate.

In the afternoon a dust storm hit us and I was choking so bad it was terrible. My mouth and nose got full of dust and I didn't have enough spit in my mouth to spit it out. One of the drags slipped down a ravine and Doom made believe he didn't even see it. I didn't say nothing to him. I just went around and looked down at the drag. It was trying to get up the ravine and I eased Pawnee down, made a small run at him, and watched him scramble back up to the trail.

I thought about Mama. She would not even believe how bad I feel. I got dirt and grime in every part of me that is open, including my ears, nose, and mouth. Even my eyes feel gritty.

When we bedded down I laid out my roll with Chubb and the remuda in case we had trouble with somebody trying to steal the horses. Chubb made coffee and told me how he had come to meet the Captain.

"I was sixteen when the war broke out and living up in the hills near Grandfather Mountain, North Carolina," he said. "I heard about the war but I did not know what it was about. They come around talking about how we was going to fight the Yankees and I asked why. They told us a lot of stuff about how the Yankees was messing with our way of life and whatnot. I didn't ever remember seeing a Yankee. Then they told us that the Yankees wanted to free all the Negroes.

"Still did not mean no whole lot to me. Anyway, they were getting rough about us joining up and fighting so I went on and did it.

"We started off all spit and grit and talking about how we was going to send the Yankees back to Boston by way of East Hell. I was on foot and I must have marched halfway through the South about nineteen or twenty times. Get up and march ten miles, then get up and march back, then run around this creek and run around this hill. It was tiresome, mighty tiresome."

"You were beating the Yankees?" I asked.

"I don't know. They was killing us and we was killing them. If you was alive at the end of the day I guess you won.

"One morning we attacked a little garrison called Milliken's Bend across from Vicksburg. They wanted that little place because it stopped us from sending cattle into Vicksburg. We pushed them back good, but it was rough going. Lord, it was some rough going.

"My company started pulling back, that is when I met

the Captain. He was pulling this body along. Heck, I saw the guy was dead, but he was asking for help getting him back to the doctor.

"I saw the look in his eyes and I knew the guy either meant a lot to him or he had just had too much of seeing people dead."

"That was his brother?"

"Yeah. Tore his heart out when that boy died. He wasn't nothing but a kid, too. 'Bout your age."

"They had black soldiers there?"

"All I saw that day was the uniforms and the bayonets," Chubb said. "I found out later there was some blacks there, but I wasn't doing no head count.

"When the war was over I asked him what he was going to do and he did not have no plans and I did not have plans and he asked me if I wanted to go to Texas. I asked him what was in Texas and he said he didn't rightly know and that made us equal so I said I would go."

I planned to wash some of the dirt off, but the next thing I knew I was waking up even though I do not remember ever going to sleep. There was some commotion going on and I listened but did not hear the sound of a stampede.

I got my gun from under my blanket roll and tried to figure out what was going on when I saw the chuck and a small band of Indians all around it. I got up on Thunder, who I had saddled nearby, and headed toward the chuck with myself as ready as I could be.

What it was was Isaiah and Timmy and some Indians they had brought back with them. The chuck was loaded with supplies and I thought the Indians wanted to take some beeves.

Then I found out what had happened. Timmy had brought back an Indian girl and he was telling the Captain he wanted to marry her.

We were all pretty surprised and gathered around to look at the girl, who was brown-skinned with dark, wide eyes. She was good looking all right and I could see how Timmy could want to marry her. When she smiled she had nice teeth. She wore a blue-and-red necklace and altogether made a good picture.

"I can take a day off to get married and then I'll catch the herd on the next day," Timmy said.

I looked at the other three Indians. There was an old man and two young braves. They did not look like they wanted trouble and I do not think that Isaiah would lead them back to camp if they did. To tell the truth they were looking poorly, with the girl being the only one of them looked like she had been eating regular.

The Captain looked at them and then he called the old

man over to one side and he talked to him. Then they called the girl over and they talked to her, and by the way her face looked she was sure happy.

Then the Captain called Jake over and spoke to him and he went over to the herd and cut out a steer.

What the Captain did was to give the Indians a choice. They could take Timmy to marry the girl or take a steer. They were happy to take the steer, which did not make Timmy feel too good.

Kansas

July 1

Isaiah had picked up some white flour and we had white bread for the first time on the trail. It was all right if you like it but it was better to look at than to eat. He had also picked up some salve, which he thought would help Pretty, and me and Chubb rubbed him down good. I think it helped a lot, but he was still wheezing.

We are in Kansas.

July 2

Timmy still has a bad case of tight jaws because the Captain gave the Indians a steer instead of letting him get married. Some more Indians came by and they were begging for beeves or anything else they could get and you could see they were in a bad way, too. One of them had a letter, which Jake called me over to read. It said that these were good Indians and they could use some help and maybe a steer or two. It was signed Will Jenkins. When I read that to the Captain he had us cut two of Jenkins's steers, the ones we had added to the herd, to give to the Indians.

July 3

"Your horse is waiting for you, boy."

That was what the Captain said when I come in to have breakfast. I was riding Blade so I knew he was not talking about him.

I went over to the remuda and Chubb was roping out horses for the day's trail.

"He's suffering," Chubb said.

I went over to where Pretty was half sitting down. When he saw me he got to his feet and I could see it was a real struggle. Chubb came up behind me and handed me his rifle.

O Lord, it was the worst thing I ever had to do in my life. I put a bridle on Pretty and walked with him. The land was flat and you could see for just miles around and we walked, Pretty and me, real slow to where there were some trees. I told Pretty that I really loved him, that there was no other horse in the world that I would ever love as much as him, and I think he knew I was telling the truth.

When we got to where the trees were I thought of having Pretty walk on ahead but when I let the bridle go he stayed right with me. I took him behind the trees and he laid down and I sat down with him and held his head and ran my fingers through his mane. I did not want him to look at me because if he had seen how I looked with the tears running down my face he might have thought he had done something wrong, which he had not. I thought about how I had sung to the cattle at night and got them calmed down, and thought about singing to Pretty. I got out a few words of "Lorena," but I couldn't go on with it.

I told him I was sorry and then I stood up with the rifle. Pretty tried to stand up, but I patted his neck and he laid down again. He was really suffering bad, and I had known it for a while. I said a prayer for him and then I used the rifle.

I will not be in this business for very long. I think I will get some more book learning and maybe teach school or look for a job on a farm.

I do not want to be around no more cattle and no more horses.

July 4

Nobody is talking to nobody. Everybody is too tired and too dirty and too sore and too discouraged. I am trying not to think about Pretty but I think about him night and day. I did not want to see him suffer but I did not want to see him die, either.

Isaiah came over and told me that Pretty had been a

fine horse and I had been a good rider for him. I was going to say something nice about Pretty, but it didn't get out of my throat.

July 6

Saw a man selling buffalo hides from a wagon. They were piled high and they stunk.

"You air them out good and they stop stinking after a while," he said.

"What did you do with the rest of the buffaloes?" I asked.

"Left them for the coyotes or whatever else is out there," he said.

The buffalo hunter, which was what the guy was, stunk as bad as the hides, maybe even worse. The Captain said the government bought a lot of the hides. It was a way of controlling the Indians, he said. He knew a lot.

July 7

I had never been as far north as Kansas and I wanted to see just what the people looked like. Well, they did not look any different from Texas people. I had borrowed a saddle from Chubb. It wasn't new but it was different. The difference was that the leather was softer and did not creak when you rode and was a lot easier on the sitting-down area.

I was used to riding Thunder and we had come to an understanding, but he would never replace Pretty in my heart.

July 8

We have made good time, but another herd is moving up on us and the Captain does not want them to pass or get too close and have our herds mix, so we are still pushing.

July 12

We bought two chickens and some eggs from a farmer and he threw in some onions and Isaiah made all of it at noon and it was delicious.

July 14

I think this is Mama's birthday. Happy birthday, Mama, if it is. And happy day if it's just a regular day!

We are holding the herd at Holland Creek, waiting for Mr. Muhlen. There is good grazing here and the Captain said that we will stay here four or five days so the herd will look good when they go into Abilene. He told us to get some rest because we would have some hard work to do in a few days.

Timmy told me his grandfather came from Ireland and was a pig farmer over there. He got to Louisiana and worked on a fishing boat. He thought they did not have pigs in Louisiana, because he did not see any for the first two years he was here.

"My daddy had five brothers," Timmy said, "and he hated fishing so he picked up and came over to Mexico and worked on a ranch until Texas broke off from Mexico in the war. He had a little farm, but it did not make any money and between raids from the Mexicans and raids from the Indians he could barely stay alive. When a guy brought a herd through and said they were looking for hands my father gave me two dollars and a saddle and told me to do the best I could."

Mr. Muhlen came and told us that the herd was looking good and that we had done a good job. That made everybody feel good, but we were anxious to get on with finishing the job.

"Your mama will be glad you are feeling so good," he said to me. "Except that she might not recognize you. You are two shades blacker and as raggedy as a scarecrow in a thunderstorm. You look like you have been riding shotgun on Rough Row for the last two months."

In truth I did not look too good. I borrowed the mirror

that Isaiah kept in the chuck and looked myself over and saw that I was sunbaked a deep black and had enough dirt on me to be mistaken for something thrown away.

The word was that Mr. Muhlen had sold the herd for a good price and we were just waiting for our time to get into Abilene and load the cattle onto trains.

I tried to get myself fixed up ready to go into Abilene. My pants were shiny in the back and pretty threadbare and my shirt was torn. It was covered by the vest I wore, so it did not look too bad.

When the word came to move the herd closer to Abilene we saw another herd coming toward us. There was a huge cloud of dust and me and Billy Steele climbed a tree to see what we could see. The herd coming went on for as far as we could see and there was another herd beyond that.

Just outside of Abilene we walked the herd to a corral that was the biggest I had ever seen. Mr. Muhlen brought some men to see the herd and they walked around the corral a little and they gave us the slant eye and then they shook hands with Mr. Muhlen and I guess the deal was done.

Handling a steer on the open range was hard because they are big and strong and can put a horn in you faster than you can blink. But loading those steers into the chutes leading to the trains was no piece of cake.

What we had to do was to line up outside the chutes and get the cattle moving in the right direction by poking at them with sticks. Sometimes they would run like crazy through the chutes, just about tearing down the railing, and you had to calm them down and get them walking right. But you could not get any part of you over the rail in case they banged into the sides or in case one took a notion to jump the rail. When they were not trying to stampede they would just stop cold and sit down or try to turn around and come out the same way they went in. Then you would have to hit them with a whip or a doubled-up rope and poke them with the sticks and rods and hope that they took to it kindly.

It took half the day for us to load the herd into a freight train and it might have been the longest half day I have spent. A lot of other cowboys helped us and some people working for the train company, which was the Kansas Pacific.

When we finished loading Mr. Muhlen's herd we were done and Jake started whooping and yelling and we all did. The train started pulling out and as soon as it did another train started pulling in and another herd started moving in.

I felt proud that I had come all the way from Texas without messing up. I had got the job done. Like a man should.

July 15

We camped down near Mud Creek and for the first time since May we did not have guard duty at night. I did not get a bit of sleep because I was still listening for the herd. It was a funny feeling not to have those cattle around and I wondered if they felt the same about us.

"When I draw my pay I am going to let Abilene know I have arrived," Timmy said, which sounded like a good idea to me and I said I would do the same.

The Captain told us the chuck was going to stay with us for four days until Mr. Muhlen finished his business. We could each have three dollars in advance until we got paid, which would probably be the next day or so.

I was all ready to get myself into Abilene, when the Captain told me and Jake we had to stay with the horses.

Down from where we were there was a row of cabins and some long, low houses and there was some activity going on there and I could see from where I was that some of the people there were women.

"Women love soldiers and cowboys," Jake said.

He went on talking about how he had had a sweetheart in Alabama and another one in Georgia during the war. But all I was thinking of was how I wanted to get into town and see what there was to see. As far as I was concerned it was high time to put on a man's boots and have Abilene take a look at me.

Later

Me, Timmy, and Jake went to town, and each of us had our three dollars' draw money from the Captain. He told us the three dollars would not be held against our wages, which made us all feel pretty good because it was free money and we planned to spend it. The first thing we did was go into a restaurant. We ordered lunch and this is what I got:

- ~ Two eggs
- ~ One piece of bacon
- ~ Some runny grits
- ~ Two biscuits and a cup of coffee

"You boys been out all night?" the girl serving up the food asked. She was pretty and had her lips painted. Timmy said she sounded like a Georgia girl.

When we had finished eating the grub she brought over a napkin for each of us and said that the bill would be fifty cents apiece. I nearly fell over when she said fifty cents. I could not imagine such lousy grub costing that much.

We went outside and looked around the town. It was early in the morning, but everything was open already. I told Timmy and Jake about what Doom had said about being a man, at least most of it.

"There are three things you have to do to be a man," Timmy said. "You have to shoot straight, lie with a straight face, and kiss a beautiful woman. Have you ever kissed a beautiful woman, Josh?"

"Yes, I have," I said.

"Well," Timmy said, "I see you have got the lying with a straight face down pat."

Then he and Jake had a big laugh on me and I had to smile myself.

We were supposed to meet Mr. Muhlen at twelve o'clock at the Drover's Cottage Hotel, so we had some time to just walk around the town. Well, it is the biggest town I have ever seen in my life, with bars and hotels and just about anything else a man could fix his mind to think on. Some girls saw us walking down the street and walked up to us just as nice as you please and asked us if they could show us around the town. Timmy said yes and they asked if we would buy them a drink over at the Bull's Head Café and we said we did not have any money unless the drinks cost a nickel apiece. They asked what had happened to our money and we told them we had not got paid yet.

"Be sure to come see us at the Bull's Head Café when you get paid," one of the girls said.

Jake said they were fancy ladies and I said I did not know if they were or not.

I saw a sign that said McLEAN'S BLACKSMITH AND HORSE DOCTOR so I went over and saw the man there. I told him how Pretty had been sick and asked if he thought he could have done anything for him.

"Where is he now?" he asked.

I told him and he said that he could not do anything for a dead horse and told me not to waste his time. I felt mad about what he said. Then he called me back and said it sounded like I had done the right thing.

"Hey, what are you boys doing sporting guns in town?" a fellow asked.

"Same as you," Timmy said.

"I am with the law," the fellow said. "Jim Gainsford is the name and I am telling you no guns are allowed in Abilene."

We said we were supposed to meet Mr. Muhlen at Drover's and if he said we would have to put up our guns we would do so, but if he did not say so we would not.

"You go over there and find him, then," the fellow said. "Because if you do not put your guns up we will have to take them from you dead or alive."

"That sounds good to me," Jake said. "And you will be a good man if you can reach out of your grave and take my gun."

We went over to Drover's Cottage with that fellow

right behind us. When we got inside we asked a man at the desk for Mr. Muhlen and he pointed to a sign that said ALL GUNS MUST BE CHECKED.

Then another fellow, all dressed up like a drawing in a picture book with a yellow vest and fancy pants, came over. He was at least six feet tall and had hair down to his shoulders like a woman. He also had a Colt riding high on his belt.

"My name is Bill Hickok," he said. "I am the marshal here in Abilene and I do not allow no guns in town. So if you will kindly put yours up on the counter and take them when you are ready to hit the trail I will be obliged."

Just then the Captain and Mr. Muhlen come through the doors from one of the back rooms. Mr. Muhlen came over and asked what was the matter and he was told. Then he said for us to put our guns up until we were ready to leave town. I saw that the Captain did not have on his gun.

We did not have the herd, we did not have our jobs to do, and now we did not have our guns. It was a miserable feeling for a little while, but only for a little while.

"Go look around the town, boys," the Captain said. "I will see you at noon. Be careful, though. Abilene can be rougher than the trail."

We went down the street until we met a Negro who

was playing a banjo and saying that everybody should go see a new place called Tom Downey's Café and get a free drink. Since it was the only thing free we had seen we went over there. We sat down and a man asked us what we wanted. Jake said he wanted a whiskey and me and Timmy each had a glass of iced tea. That is when our first troubles broke out.

"Gunfight!" That was what somebody shouted and the whole bar cleared out to go see what was going on.

When we got outside there was Doom getting into a jawing contest with a short whiny-voiced dude sporting a big mustache and a gun he had strapped to his leg real low.

"That's Wes Hardin. He's killed more people than he has said howdy to," a big fellow said.

Doom was still toting his gun and he was keeping his hand by his side. There were a lot of rough-looking cowhands on the street and most of them were moving out of the line of fire.

"Here comes that marshal," Timmy said.

The marshal came walking up slow with two men wearing badges right behind him. My mouth went dry because I thought for sure that somebody was going to die. The marshal looked at the man they called Hardin and turned his head to one side.

"Is he worth the killing, Wes?" the marshal asked.

"Maybe you ought to ask him if he is ready to die," Doom said.

The marshal pulled out his gun real slow and told Doom to kindly take his hat off. Doom looked at the marshal and at Hardin and reached to take it off.

"Throw it down on the ground," Hickok said.

Seeing that the marshal had his gun out and was wearing a badge, Doom let his hat drop to the ground. No sooner had he dropped it than the marshal put a hole through it.

Doom took a step back. His mouth was working and I knew he was thinking about going for his gun.

"Wes, does that look like a one-hole hat to you?" the marshal asked.

That fellow pulled his gun out so fast you could hardly see it and before you knew it Doom's hat was skipping down the street.

Then the marshal went and took Doom's gun from him and walked away without saying nary a word.

Wes Hardin looked at Doom and spit on the ground. Then he turned around and walked away, too.

"You are one lucky cowboy," a cowhand said. "That man wakes up in the morning itching to kill somebody."

They were playing life a lot cheaper than I had a mind to, and I was glad I didn't have my gun.

I walked all over Abilene and saw everything a man

could see, including two cowboys who had saddled mules and raced them down the street.

Afternoon

We went back over to Drover's Cottage to see if Mr. Muhlen was there yet and he was. All the guys were there except Chubb and Billy, who were watching the horses. Mr. Muhlen took us into a side room and counted out the money for each man.

"What are you going to do with your money, Joshua?" he asked me.

I had not thought about it but then I did and figured out that I did not know except to give most of it to Mama. I told him that.

"How much you want to give her?" he asked. "I will take it back to her for you."

I knew Mr. Muhlen was a good man and a man of his word. All the money I had earned, along with the bonus, came out to be eighty dollars. I asked him to take back sixty dollars and I would keep twenty. He counted out the money and told me to keep both my eyes open and my mind the same. He also said that he admired a man who took care of his mother.

Afterward we all stood outside feeling pretty good. Isaiah said he was going to get drunk and Wade said he was going to have more fun than he had ever had in his whole life and buy him some new boots, a new saddle, and maybe a hat.

"Not with the way things cost here in Abilene," Chubb said.

I was looking for somebody to pal around with and Timmy was looking for the same so we went down together to a place that was called the Novelty Theater and looked in. There were some people standing around and when they asked us to come back later to see a show we said we would.

Then we went over to the Frontier store and looked at some of the fancy duds and stuff they had over there. Everything they had in the store was as bright as a new penny and to tell the truth the money I had drawn was burning a hole in my pocket. The ropes were stiff with fancy loops at the ends which the Mexicans called *hondas*, made out of tying colored rawhide around the end of the rope. It looked fancy, but I didn't think it was going to last if you worked it. What I picked out was a blue shirt with pockets and fancy workings on it and also a new pair of pants with side stripes like Mexican pants. That cost nine dollars, which left me only eleven dollars from my main money and fifty cents from the three dollars' draw money. I was thinking about going to find Mr. Muhlen and asking him for more of my money. But he had gone on so much about how good I was to my mama I felt bad about it.

Timmy bought a new saddle, a slouch hat, and a new holster, which was the nicest-looking holster I had ever seen. I wished I had bought that instead of the shirt and pants, even though I did need the pants something terrible.

Later we went over to see the show.

The show was one dollar, which most everything in Abilene was, and it was with a man playing piano and some people on the stage acting out a play about something. I looked around at the cowboys watching the show and they seemed to like it so I guess it was all right.

It was getting late and Timmy was thinking about staying in a hotel and we went over to see how much it would cost — fifty cents for a bed and another fifty cents for a bath. We weren't that tired or that dirty so we said no.

We found Miguel and he asked Timmy to lend him five dollars. Timmy asked him what had happened to his money and he said he had lost it all in a monte card game.

We went and watched the monte game, which was in the Alamo. Mr. Hickok was there playing cards and looking as pleased as a bullfrog in a horsefly roundup. Timmy played for a dollar and lost that dollar faster than you could blink.

Jake and Wade had teamed up and we found them with Jake helping Wade down the street. He had got into a fight with three guys from Montana over a girl they were all in love with and had come out on the short end.

"Well, where are the guys?" Timmy asked. He was spoiling for a fight.

"They got thrown in jail for breaking up the piano in the bar," Jake said.

Timmy decided to try out the hotel, mostly because he had never stayed in a hotel before, and I decided to go back to camp. In truth I was a little disappointed because I had let Mr. Muhlen take all my money and I was not having much fun in Abilene. I took Timmy's stuff back to camp and both Billy and Chubb asked me if I would take their guard. Billy offered me five dollars and Chubb did the same and I said I would take it for free because I did not think it was right to take money from somebody on our crew. But they had to flip for it and Chubb won. He duded up good and went off to town and me and Billy were on guard with the horses.

The long and short of it was that as towns went, Abilene was a stampede and the only things being milled was us cowboys. None of us came out of Abilene wearing a blue ribbon.

July 16

Isaiah did not show up and nobody knew where he was so we went into what supplies was left and made fixings for ourselves. By nightfall Miguel had come in and he was broke, Chubb was broke, Doom was broke, and Wade had only four dollars. Isaiah come in the morning and he was broke, too, but he was not miserable like the rest of them.

"Me and Abilene had a good time and now we are ready to lay ourselves down and get some rest," he said.

He might have been ready to get some rest, but I do not think the town of Abilene ever rested.

When I saw what had happened to everybody else I thought that I had not been so bad off. Doom was lucky to be alive the way that Hardin fellow could shoot. But I also remembered the Captain had said that Doom was going to get himself killed. Almost everybody else was broke or nearly so and all the work we had done was over and if you had not let Mr. Muhlen keep some of your money you had nothing to show for it.

Still, Abilene was an exciting place to be in. It was like drawing out your gun to shoot off one shot and have the whole five shoot at one time. It made a big bang and was a little dangerous, but you sure did not forget it in a hurry.

When I looked at all the guys sitting around feeling

miserable or talking about what they had done, I made up my mind again that I would not stay in the life of being a cowboy.

July 17

Mr. Muhlen sent a black fellow out to our camp who called himself George Glenn. He said he and Isaiah was to stay with the horses and the rest of us was to go back over to meet Mr. Muhlen.

Mr. Muhlen came in and he was dressed right fine and made us all feel proud of him. The Captain was with Mr. Muhlen but he was dressed regular except for a clean shirt. The first thing they did was to take Doom over to the bar and buy him a drink. Then Mr. Muhlen walked him to the door and I knew he was not going to be with our crew anymore.

Then Mr. Muhlen thanked the rest of us for doing a good job and gave each man a hearty handshake.

"I am asking you boys to go back down and pick up a herd near Goliad," he said. "I will pay the same wage as you have just received and if you get this herd back up here in time you will each get a ten-dollar gold piece from me. The Captain is only taking hands he wants so you should be able to handle a bigger herd."

That made me feel good and before I knew it I was

talking to Timmy about working on my roping. Being a cowboy had been a dream for me when I was back on the ranch in Texas. Now I was right in the middle of that dream and riding high.

July 18

We broke up the camp and me and Timmy rode with Chubb and the remuda and the others rode on ahead. When we broke for lunch I asked the Captain if he had really said I was a good cowboy.

"I said it and I meant it," he said. "But don't go buying no bigger hat size, 'cause you still got a lot to learn."

He didn't crack a smile when he said it, and he didn't reach out and shake my hand, neither. In a way I would have been surprised if he had done so because he is not that kind of man. I had learned a lot about what it took to go on the trail with a herd and what it meant to work with other hands and most of it I learned from the Captain. I think the Captain learned something, too. There were lots of cowhands in Abilene but he had taken on George, who looked like he had more than cow chips for brains, and who was a Negro.

August 18

Mama was really glad to see me and I was glad to see her. She said I looked as skinny as a rail and I guess I did. Mr. Muhlen had already been there and given her the money and she was pleased about that.

"I got a letter from your father," she said.

I knew Mama could not read, so I got the letter. She sat me down at the table and looked dead at me to make sure I was reading what was in the letter. I knew if I did not read it right she would know.

Dear Kissee,

I am writing this letter to you from Harpers Ferry, Virginia, where I have found some work keeping the tracks clear but it does not pay enough to do more than get by. I hear there is work down in Big Bend where they are making a tunnel and I think I will go down there. I miss you very much. I cannot wait to send for you and Joshua. Maybe I can get him a job working on the tunnel when I see how things are.

Your loving husband,
Nehemiah Lopee

Mama acted like she was glad to hear what was in the letter, but that night I heard her crying in her sleep and I knew things were hard on her. I was even more glad I could give her the money.

August 27

Mr. Muhlen bought 1,750 head of cattle from Mexico and we spent the last two days working to get them ready for the trail, which meant mostly putting a trail brand on them. We are waiting for another herd that our crew is bringing over from Goliad. Meanwhile me, Chubb, Timmy, and the new Negro teamed up with some Mexicans to chase down some mustangs. Well, those mustangs are a lot smarter than cattle. We ran them and ran them, keeping them away from water as much as we could, and just about running ourselves into early graves from all the exhaustion, but it took six days to get them even near the corral trap we had built. When we got them headed for the trap we ran right up on them. They were tired and run-down from not having water and for the first time we got them going toward the trap in the early morning.

We got twenty-two horses in the trap and you could see that there was a lot of life in those animals. The Captain said we would need fifteen horses broke and ready to go in five days, when we started trailing north.

That was the first time I knew when he expected the rest of the herd to be together and us to be ready to move out.

When all the animals got to the south range and the yearlings and cows were cut out, we had to brand them and put on earmarks.

Branding that many animals is hard work and you don't get through the day without some iron burns, some rope burns, and a whole lot of bruises and scrapes, so I was just as glad to be working with the broncos.

The men rounding up the broncs naturally had first choice and I looked over the new animals carefully. I spotted a quick, good-looking runner with smart moves and a big rump and I thought he was the one with my name on his flank.

Chubb was good with horses and so were the Mexicans, and I did not want to show up the worst with a horse. When it was my turn to pick out a horse and the one I liked was still unpicked, I went after him. I roped him around his forelegs and he just kept going and jerked that rope out of my hands.

Chubb roped him around the neck and brought him to a stop. I got to him as quick as I could, slid off Pawnee, and went up to him and got my rope, which was on the ground. He was still bucking and fighting as I got ready to rope him again.

I roped his front legs again and jerked him down.

Chubb came up and twisted his head back while I tied down his back legs. He was wild-eyed and breathing hard and after I made sure that the ropes would not burn him or hurt him I had Chubb turn him loose.

"He's a fighter," Chubb said as the colt pushed to his feet.

He was brown, almost red, and I was wondering if he was four or five. It took us another half hour to hobble the other mustangs and we led them back the forty miles or so to Mr. Muhlen's ranch. Mr. Muhlen had heard what had happened to Pretty and he asked me what I was going to name the new horse.

"Lobo," I said. "That sounds like a good name."

I spent two days letting Lobo get used to me, more than with the other horses we were breaking. I rubbed him down with some quilting I got from Mama and let him try out different kinds of hobbles before I even showed him a saddle. By the third day he was used to seeing my face and hearing my voice and he knew I was not going to hurt him.

Chubb got bit bad when he tried to slip a rope into his horse's mouth and he took it out on the horse, jerking him around something awful. I knew he was not going to get a cow horse out of that animal. Me and Lobo worked together for the next week and I got him saddled six times without having to hobble him. The only real trouble I had was leading him and I had to pull him pretty good when I wanted him to follow me but I kept talking to him and rubbing his forehead and down on his eyes.

I trimmed Lobo's tail the day before we started off. I thought I had better ride him every day to make sure he was all right and used to it because sometimes if you break a horse and he doesn't get ridden right away he has to be broken in all over again, and you cannot break a horse on the trail and work with him, too.

September 1

We moved out today with me and Miguel on swing the same as we were before. We had a lot more cattle than we had on the first trip and the same amount of men to drive them. It looked like hard work coming up. But I knew it was something I wanted to do.

"When I get to Abilene I am going to get my mustache trimmed and my hair slicked down," Timmy said. "Then I am going to get some fancy duds like that Marshal Hickok."

"I'm going to buy a pearl-handled Colt pistol," Miguel said. "How about you, Joshua?"

"I am going to buy a beaver hat and some solid-silver spurs," I said, which just about topped them all.

The first time I rode Lobo at night I told him that when

I got to Abilene I was going to sleep one night in a hotel and take a fancy bath and would buy him a special blanket all his own. It was a clear night and I sang "O Mary, Don't You Weep," the same as I had on the start of my first drive. Lobo acted like he liked that song, and I thought I would save it special, just for him.

Epilogue

Between the years of 1871 and 1882 Joshua Loper made eight more drives for the Slash M Ranch: six from Texas to Kansas and two from Texas to Wyoming. In 1883 he was the trail boss on a drive from Texas to Ellsworth, Kansas, when the news reached him that Mr. Muhlen had died. Later that year Mrs. Muhlen sold the Slash M to an Englishman named Carty. Joshua decided it was time to move on and found a job as a stock manager with the Kansas Pacific Railway in Kansas City. He worked for the Kansas Pacific until the summer of 1886.

In the fall of 1886 he traveled to Chicago, where he visited a number of meatpacking plants and began working for P. D. Armour as an agent. In this capacity he bought cattle from ranchers for eastern markets.

Also in 1886, Joshua met Carrie Lynch, a schoolteacher from Nashville, Tennessee, who was on her way to visit her aunt in Nicodemus, Kansas. They fell in love and were married in September of 1886 and had their first child, Samuel Loper, in July of 1887. Joshua and Carrie returned to Texas, where Carrie started a school for Colored children in Fort Worth, and Joshua continued to work as an agent for the meatpacker.

Joshua's father, Nehemiah, settled in Littig, Texas, in 1872, where he owned and operated a general store and later became postmaster. Joshua's mother, Kissee, moved to Littig in September of 1872 to be with her husband. Nehemiah died in 1898, and Kissee died two years later, in 1900. Both were buried in Littig.

Timmy O'Hara moved to Denison, Texas, where he started a feed business. He and Joshua wrote to each other at least twice a year until Tim moved to Oklahoma, which had been Indian Territory, in 1908.

Captain James Hunter took herds north until 1880. In 1881 he settled for a while in Cincinnati, Ohio, where he tried running a store. He then accepted a job running a ranch in Santiago, Cuba. He was killed on the Fourth of July, 1898, while fighting against American troops during the Spanish-American War.

Isaiah Cotton moved to Philadelphia, Pennsylvania, where he became a cook in the Blue Dolphin Seafood Restaurant.

By the beginning of the First World War, the heyday of the cowboy had ended, and Joshua saw his son become the successful owner of several barbershops in Austin, Texas.

Joshua Loper died in his sleep on March 15, 1920. He was sixty-three years old. His journal was not found until after the death of his wife, Carrie, who died on September 2, 1933. It was found in a big envelope with an old Civil War pouch and a tattered neckerchief. The envelope was labeled COWBOY STUFF.

Life in America
in 1871

Historical Note

Before the beginning of the Civil War in 1860, the cattle that were taken to market were used for their hides, which were used to make leather items and tallow for candles. Few Americans ate beef. In fact, in 1854, when a herd of cattle was brought from Texas all the way to New York City, the *New York Tribune* ran a story about the taste of cow.

However, when the war ended conditions were right for the rapid growth of the West's livestock industry. The eastern part of the United States had been heavily settled for decades, but the land west of the Mississippi was largely unsettled. Three million cattle roamed freely across the open ranges of northern Mexico and Texas. Very few were taken for food.

These cattle, first brought to the New World by the Spanish, ran in wild herds primarily south of the Rio Grande. They belonged to no one. To develop the livestock industry a market for the beef was needed, as well as men willing to sell them to the market, and other men to round up the wild herds and somehow get them to the markets. The men rounding up the cattle and taking them on the long drives were the cowboys.

Entrepreneurs, men who were skillful in selling products, came to the West and saw the herds of free-roaming cattle. They knew that there were markets for them in the northern and eastern sections of the United States.

A strong factor in the growth of the livestock industry was the railroad. By 1869 railroads stretched across the United States from California to New England. There were large rail yards in Kansas through which cattle could be loaded and brought quickly to warehouses in Chicago and New York. Getting the animals to the rail yards would never be an easy chore. The cattle could not be moved more than ten to fifteen miles per day. A faster pace would make the animals unfit to market. They had to have large amounts of water each day and so the trails they took had to include watering places. Along with these responsibilities, the cowboy had to be an expert horseman and be willing to risk his life to stop a stampede, fight it out with rustlers, and work for long hours without sleep.

The first cowboys in North America were the young men who rounded up cattle in Mexico, riding horses descended from those brought from Spain hundreds of years before by the conquistadores. Many of the words that came into the language of the cowboy had come from the Spanish. *Vaquero*, which in Spanish means "cowboy," was transformed into the term "buckaroo." The Spanish term for "the rope" was *la reata*, which became "lariat" in English. The heavy leather leg coverings, *chaperreras*, became "chaps." The *rodeo*, or cattle roundup, came to mean the test or demonstration of cowboys' skills.

Some of the first American cowboys were also of Mexican descent. Others were white Americans who had lived in Texas or who had come to Texas after fighting in the Civil War. Still others were young African Americans, many of whom had been slaves.

In 1867 American cowboys — white, Mexican, black, and some Indians — began rounding up cattle to drive north to the railheads in Kansas. It was a tough job, and most of the men who rode the trails were both rugged and young. The usual pay was a dollar a day. A man could make nearly a hundred dollars if he survived the three-month trek from the Brazos River in Texas to the stockyards in Abilene, Kansas.

But for men who had returned from the war to ruined farms and who often could not read or write, the job of cowboy was a blessing. It was a way of scratching out a living, of eating three meals a day in the open air, of using one's skills to prove oneself as the United States rebuilt itself.

For the African-American cowboy the opportunity was exceptional. There were not many opportunities for the newly freed African Americans. The Ku Klux Klan had been organized in 1866 to reestablish the dominance of the prewar plantation society. African-American soldiers who had fought for the Union during the Civil War were especially despised and many were forced from their homes. Few of these veterans were able to find jobs other than tenant farming. Still, many young African Americans did work in the newly forming cattle industry. It is estimated that one out of every three cowboys was either Mexican or African American. African Americans worked alongside their white counterparts as equals. They participated in the rounding up of wild cattle, the branding, the breaking of horses, and the long drive northward.

By 1871 the number of cattle driven from Mexico and Texas to Kansas had increased to six hundred thousand, seventeen times the amount taken on the trail just five years earlier. Beef was being shipped to markets in New York and Boston and, increasingly, across the ocean to Great Britain and Europe. To accomplish this, thousands of cowboys rode the hardy horses, often for as long as sixteen hours a day.

The towns associated with the cattle drives became

famous in their own right. Abilene, Dodge City, and Wichita were all towns situated near the end of the trail. These cow towns were wild places where nearly anything went. Many cowboys had never seen cities this large. Few had ever had more money than the eighty to ninety dollars they had been paid for bringing the cattle to Kansas. They were young men ready to blow off steam. They all carried guns and were ready to use them to raise a little hell or to quickly settle a dispute. Saloons were opened, hotels were built, gambling halls hummed with the music of the day. Young girls brought in from all over the country winked at the cowboys and at the law.

Just as the eastern markets had created the cattle industry, the cow towns created the legendary gunfighters. Men like Wes Hardin, Doc Holliday, the Earps, and James "Wild Bill" Hickok became the heroes of the Wild West, whose exploits filled eastern newspapers.

By 1880 the glory of the cowboy had begun to fade. Wild cattle were being replaced by heavier, more profitable, domesticated cattle. Railroads became more efficient, and meat-processing plants were being built closer to the source of the livestock. As the business of the livestock industry became more sophisticated, the need for the cowboy gradually decreased. By 1890 the job of the cowboy had become less significant to the industry.

Still, cowboys remain an important part of American

history. For many Americans, and for much of the world, they represent the strength and individualism that made America special. African Americans were a major part of this strength, this spirit of determination and ruggedness.

Most Americans today know only the Hollywood version of the cowboy. If there is more to know, it is simply this: The faces of the men were more diverse than Hollywood has shown, the work was harder, and the cowboys tougher.

In order to meet the growing market for beef in the East, more and more cowboys, like these shown in Frank Tenney Johnson's Riders of the Dawn, *were needed. Cowboys were tough, rugged young men of varied backgrounds. Some were of Mexican descent, like the first cowboys in North America; some were Caucasian; others were African American or Indian.*

Of the estimated thirty-five thousand cowboys who worked the ranches and rode the trails in the late 1800s, between five and nine thousand or more were black. A large portion of black cowboys were former slaves and sons of slaves who traveled to the West after the Civil War in search of opportunity. They participated in almost all of the drives northward, and were assigned to almost every job.

After mustangs for the drive were captured on the open range, men who specialized in breaking horses went to work, charging five dollars a head. A good horseman could break several horses in a week, working with each horse every day until it was tame enough to be turned over to the ranch's regular cowboys.

Cowboys were responsible for rounding up the cattle and taking them to one of the large cattle towns, such as Abilene, Kansas, where they would be shipped to market. Before taking the herd to trail, cowboys branded their cattle and horses to establish ownership. Brands, which are made up of letters of the alphabet, numerals, and designs of familiar objects, were sometimes altered by cattle rustlers, who would then claim that they owned the animals. Here, rustlers dispute a longhorn's brand.

Cowboys gathered at the chuck wagon to talk about their day, tell stories, sing songs, and eat meals of beef stew, beans, and bread. The chuck wagon contained food, water, and almost everything else the cowboys might need during the roundup and drive. Cooking utensils, some food, and "medicinal" whiskey were held in the rear cabinet, while bulk food, guns, tobacco, and bedrolls were kept in the wagon bed.

143

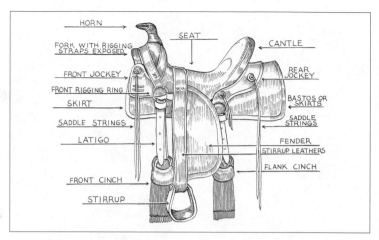

This illustration shows the parts of a Western saddle. The lighter saddles used by Texans were far better for working cattle than the hornless ones often used by northern cattle raisers.

When the Texans arrived on the northern ranges, the often intense wind made it hard to keep their wide-brimmed hats on their heads. They eventually adopted the narrow-brimmed hats worn by the northern cowboys. This illustration shows hats ranging from the poblanos *worn by the Mexican cowboys to the high-crowned, wide-brimmed hat that is popular today.*

144

A.R. Waud's illustration of Texas longhorns crossing a stream appeared in Harper's Weekly. *River crossings were especially dangerous to cowboys who couldn't swim. If cattle were swept downstream, men and horses could be lost or drowned.*

Longhorns were restless by nature, and anything from a prairie dog to the rumble of distant thunder could start a stampede, which could last for hours, leaving cattle scattered across the range. To stop the stampede, cowboys turned the head cattle and made them run in an increasingly tight circle. This forced them to slow down and eventually stop. Sadly, stampedes often resulted in the deaths of both cowboys and cattle.

145

Between 1867 and 1871, cowboys drove a million and a half Texas longhorns along the Chisholm Trail to Abilene, Kansas, a stop on the Kansas–Pacific Railroad. This engraving depicts cowboys loading cattle on a train for shipment to eastern markets.

When cowboys reached the railhead after months on a dusty trail, a haircut and a bath were their first order of business. Once clean, the cowboys headed out to spend their earnings on clothes, guns, gambling, and women. M. Goldsoll's store in Ellsworth, Kansas, sold everything from groceries to diamonds.

This illustration from Harper's Weekly *shows Wichita, Kansas, in the early 1870s, during its period as a thriving cow town.*

Bill Pickett, a black cowboy, was most famous for inventing bulldogging, or steer wrestling. Pickett would jump onto a running steer, twist its head, bite its lip, and pull the steer to the ground. Competing in the virtually all-white Wild West shows, Pickett is said to have performed the feat over five thousand times during his lifetime. Bill Pickett was the first black honoree of the National Rodeo Hall of Fame.

148

Ben Hodges was a notorious con man, card cheat, and cattle rustler in Dodge City, Kansas.

Cowboy, gunslinger, Indian fighter, and teller of tall tales, ex-slave Nat Love claimed to have won the title of "Deadwood Dick" in a roping contest in Deadwood, South Dakota, in 1876.

Abilene, Kansas, was a rough town, but not quite as rough as Wild West legends would have it. In 1871, during his eight months as Abilene's marshal, James Butler "Wild Bill" Hickok shot and killed only two men, one of them—a fellow peace officer—by accident. Between 1870 and 1885, there were only forty-five documented homicides in five major Kansas cattle towns—Abilene, Ellsworth, Dodge City, Wichita, and Caldwell—many of which were unrelated to the cattle trade.

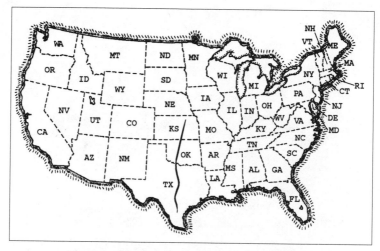

This map of the United States shows the Chisholm Trail.

About the Author

WALTER DEAN MYERS chose to write about Joshua Loper because of the important role black cowboys played in American history and because of the equality and freedom they enjoyed along with the other cowboys. It was important for Mr. Myers to depict Joshua as a vital part, and not merely a victim, of our country's history. Mr. Myers says, "Black cowboys operated in one of the most exciting eras of American history. For many they were dealing not only with the hardships of the cattle drives but with a newfound freedom as well. They were being allowed to be *men*, to test their strength and courage against the elements, against rustlers, against anything they found along the trails from Texas to the railroads."

Walter Dean Myers is an award-winning writer of fiction, nonfiction, and poetry for young people. His many books include *Slam!*; *Somewhere in the Darkness*; *Fallen Angels*, winner of the Coretta Scott King Award; *Malcolm X: By Any Means Necessary*, a Coretta Scott King Honor

Book and ALA Notable Children's Book; and *The Glory Field*, an ALA Best Book for Young Adults and a Notable Children's Trade Book in the Field of Social Studies. Mr. Myers is the recipient of two awards for the body of his work: the Margaret A. Edwards Award for Outstanding Literature for Young Adults and the ALAN Award. He lives in Jersey City, New Jersey.

Acknowledgments

The author would like to thank Dr. James Hoy of Emporia State University, Emporia, Kansas, and Bertha Calloway at the Great Plains Black Museum for their assistance in preparing this book. And, of course, Amy Griffin, my editor.

Grateful acknowledgment is made for permission to reprint the following:

Cover portrait: Photo of Fondy Warton courtesy of The Paul Stewart Collection, Aurora, Colorado.

Cover background: A detail from Frank Tenney Johnson's *Riders of the Dawn*, courtesy of The Anschutz Collection.

Foldout map illustration copyright © 1999 by Bryn Bernard.

Page 141 (top): Cowboys, courtesy of The Anschutz Collection.
Page 141 (bottom): Black cowboys, LC.S611.015, *African-American Cowboys with Their Mounts Saddled Up, Posed in Connection with a Fair in Bonham, Texas, in the Interest of Interracial Relations*, Erwin E. Smith, ca. 1911–1915, nitrate negative, The Erwin E. Smith Collection of the Library of Congress on deposit at the Amon Carter Museum, Fort Worth, Texas.

Page 142: Breaking a horse, *Frank Leslie's Illustrated Newspaper, The American West in the Nineteenth Century*, Dover Publications, Inc., New York, 1992.

Page 143 (top): Frederic Remington's illustration of cowboys disputing a brand, *Ready-to-Use Old West Cuts*, Dover Publications, Inc., New York, 1995.

Page 143 (bottom): Chuck wagon, LC.S59.166, *A JA Cook Inspecting His Stew. JA Ranch, Texas*. Erwin E. Smith, negative, 1907, The Erwin E. Smith Collection of the Library of Congress on deposit at the Amon Carter Museum, Fort Worth, Texas.

Page 144 (top): Saddle, *Cowboy Culture* by David Dary, Alfred A. Knopf Inc., New York, 1981.

Page 144 (bottom): Cowboy hats, ibid.

Page 145 (top): River crossing, *Harper's Weekly, The American West in the Nineteenth Century*, Dover Publications, Inc., New York, 1992.

Page 145 (bottom): Stampede, ibid.

Page 146 (top): Loading cattle, ibid.

Page 146 (bottom): Advertisement, The Kansas State Historical Society, Topeka, Kansas.

Page 147: Wichita, Kansas, *The American West in the Nineteenth Century*, Dover Publications, Inc., New York, 1992.

Page 148: Bill Pickett, ibid.

Page 149: Ben Hodges, The Denver Public Library, Western History Collection.

Page 150: Nat Love, Schomburg Center for Research in Black Culture, New York Public Library.

Page 151: Bill Hickok, The Kansas State Historical Society, Topeka, Kansas.

Page 152: Map by Heather Saunders.

Other books in the My Name Is America series

The Journal of William Thomas Emerson
A Revolutionary War Patriot
by Barry Denenberg

The Journal of James Edmond Pease
A Civil War Union Soldier
by Jim Murphy

To Pamela Jones, who loves cowboys and children

While the events described and some of the characters in this book may be based on actual historical events and real people, Joshua Loper is a fictional character, created by the author, and his journal is a work of fiction.

Copyright © 1999 by Walter Dean Myers

Library of Congress Cataloging-in-Publication Data
Myers, Walter Dean, 1937–
The journal of Joshua Loper, a black cowboy/
by Walter Dean Myers. — 1st ed.
p. cm. — (My name is America)
Summary: In 1871, Joshua Loper, a sixteen-year-old black cowboy, records in his journal his experiences while making his first cattle drive under an unsympathetic trail boss.

ISBN 0-590-02691-7 (paper over board)

[1. Cattle drives — Fiction.   2. Cowboys — Fiction.
3. West (U.S.) — Fiction.   4. Afro-Americans — Fiction.   5. Diaries — Fiction.]
I. Title. II. Series.
PZ7.M992Jo 1999
[Fic] — dc21   98-18661
CIP   AC

10   9   8   7   6   5   4   3   2   9/9   0/0   01   02   03

The display type was set in Bostonia.
The text type was set in Berling.
Book design by Pauline Neuwirth and Elizabeth Parisi
Photo research by Zoe Moffitt
Printed in the U.S.A.   23
First edition, April 1999

MAP

of the

CHISHOLM TRAIL

across

TEXAS, OKLAHOMA & KANSAS

1871

LEGEND

• • • • • • • • • *The Chisholm Trail*

━━┿━┿━┿━━ *Railroads*

~~~~~~~~~ *Rivers*

━━━━━━ *Borders*

★ *Towns*

Red River

GULF OF MEXICO

ELLSWORTH   ABILENE

The Kansas - Pacific Railroad

K A N S A S

★ DODGE CITY   WICHITA

CALDWELL

Salt Fork of the Arkansas River   Arkansas R.

I N D I A N
T E R R I T O R Y
(O K L A H O M A)

Canadian River

C H I S H O L M   T R A I L

T E X A S

Trinity R.

Brazos River

Rio Grande

M E X I C O